A BENCHER FAMILY BOOK

RULES
OF *Negotiation*

A BENCHER FAMILY BOOK

RULES OF *Negotiation*

INARA SCOTT

Entangled Publishing, LLC
10940 S Parker Rd
Suite 327
Parker, CO 80134
rights@entangledpublishing.com

Indulgence is an imprint of Entangled Publishing, LLC.

Edited by Libby Murphy
Cover design by LJ Anderson/Mayhem Cover Creations
Cover photography by NeonShot/GettyImages

Manufactured in the United States of America

First Edition February 2012

To Libby Murphy, editor extraordinaire, for making writing fun again.

Chapter One

"Here, kitty-kitty-kitty…"

A pair of yellow eyes glared at Tori from the far rear corner of the dark, empty space under her front porch. She'd brought Fritzy home from the pound less than a year ago, in an attempt to fulfill her destiny as an unattached twenty-something creeping toward thirty. Fritzy, who had apparently been named by somebody with a fondness for all things German, was supposed to give her an outlet. He was supposed to be a vessel into which she could pour all her love and devotion, and hopefully receive something in return.

Instead, he had turned out to be an antisocial beast who resented her frequent business trips and showed his displeasure by peeing on her shoes and shredding her curtains. The pound attendant had conveniently forgotten to mention said cat was Satan with fur.

Tori tried again, crouching down and leaning into the darkness as she shook the small bag of treats intended to lure Fritzy into her arms and then into the cat carrier she'd cunningly left in the car, so he wouldn't know what was coming. Except that he *did* know what was coming. He *always* knew what was coming. Especially at 6:00 a.m., when she had to be at the airport in less than two hours.

Tori tried to keep her voice pleasant. "Here, you pain-in-the-ass monster masquerading as a cat...here, Mr. Fluffypants..."

"Tori, is that you under there?"

She straightened abruptly and hit her head on the edge of the porch. "Shit...I mean, damn it...I mean..."

Her tiny white-haired neighbor, Mrs. Jenkins, who glowed with saintly inner light and probably had never spoken the word "damn," smiled peacefully in return. "Traveling again?"

Tori nodded and unthinkingly wiped her dusty hands on her skirt, and then stared in horror at the trails of dirt left behind on the silky gray fabric. Her mind started to spin. Plane leaving at 7:55. Ten minutes to the kennel, fifty-minute drive to the Philadelphia airport, assuming there wasn't any traffic, which of course there would be. Doors closed thirty minutes before takeoff. Security would take at least twenty minutes.

Five minutes to change her skirt?

No way. She had three straight days of traveling ahead, and missing any one of her flights could send her into eternal airport purgatory. She couldn't afford that right now. Not when her trip culminated in a visit to New York City, where she hoped to lock-down the key terms of the sale of the software business owned by her client, Jerry Tollefson.

She'd been negotiating the contract for months, and knew everyone in her firm was watching—especially the partnership committee. If she screwed this up, they'd never forget it.

Not to mention that, after four years of working together, Jerry happened to be closest thing to a best friend she had.

He deserved a great deal, and she was determined to get it for him.

"Why don't you let me get Fritzy?" Mrs. Jenkins offered.

Tori watched in amazement as the fragile woman tottered to the edge of the porch. Stabilizing herself with one hand on the wooden railing, Mrs. Jenkins peered into the darkness. "Fritzy, you come here right now," she called, a hint of steel underlying her gentle voice.

A few moments later, an orange-striped tabby curled around Mrs. Jenkins's feet, mewing and rubbing his head on the old woman's orthopedic black shoes.

Tori's heart snapped. She couldn't even pretend it didn't hurt.

"I feed him tuna sometimes while you're gone," Mrs. Jenkins said, almost apologetically. "Don't feel bad. I know how busy you are. Cats are difficult, you know. They take things personally."

She blinked. "I don't know how to thank—"

Mrs. Jenkins—what *was* her first name, anyway? Tori realized she had no idea—raised a hand to stop her. "You run along and catch your plane, sweetheart. Fritzy and I will be fine."

Tori took one final look at the cat—*her* cat—sprawled lovingly on the ground in front of her neighbor, and ran for the car. She really should have gotten a pet rock instead.

· · ·

The first thing Brit Bencher, CEO of Excorp Corporation, noticed about Tori was her stance: feet slightly wide-set, shoulders flung back. A large leather purse swung over one shoulder. She held out a stack of papers in front of her.

She was determined. Confident. A worthy adversary.

Good. Brit didn't do guilt, but he did occasionally do

regret. And manipulating a woman without a decent set of defenses had the potential to leave him experiencing exactly that. The same unpleasant emotion he now carried around for having let his little sister move to California and shack up with The Asshole.

Ever since she'd found her boyfriend screwing her best friend almost a year ago, his baby sister had been mired in a deep, painful depression. Brit had persuaded her to relocate to New York in the hopes that a fresh start would help, but she seemed to slip further into her misery once she arrived. She'd been in town for four months, and other than buying groceries she barely even left her apartment.

The rest of the family said he should give her time, but whom were they kidding? At the rate she was going, she'd wither away by summer. Melissa didn't need space—she needed a job. A job would get her out of the house, give some structure to her days, and, most importantly, give her something to think about other than her prick of an ex.

Unfortunately, Melissa wasn't particularly interested in job-hunting, and the only company Brit had ever heard her talk about with any enthusiasm was Solen Labs. She'd been in the robotics industry ever since she'd finished her degree, and she was convinced that no one combined art, science, and technology like Solen. In the industry, Garth Solen was known as a demanding, even cruel, boss. But he also had a brilliant, singular mind. Everyone knew Solen Labs was going to make the next big breakthrough in artificial intelligence.

Melissa had told Brit there was no way she'd get a job there, but he'd insisted on sending them her resume anyway. Which of course gave her the opportunity to give him a huge "I told you so" when she got a call that Solen wasn't interested. Brit refused to take no for an answer. If he got Solen on the phone, he was certain he could convince him to interview Melissa. And from there, Brit had no doubt his brilliant sister would get the job.

Brit wasn't accustomed to guilt. But it was a feeling he could finally dispense with if he got what he wanted from Tori.

"I certainly hope you didn't bring me out here to waste my time." She spoke in a measured tone, strong but not strident. Still, he caught a hint—the tiniest, barest hint—of a wobble in her voice. Closer scrutiny revealed circles under her eyes, covered with a layer of makeup. The same scrutiny made it impossible not to notice that those eyes, which were the color of his favorite whiskey, were huge and doe-like.

But not vulnerable, Brit reminded himself. He wasn't going after a doe. He was going after a hunter. Someone like him.

He opened his mouth to speak, but she continued. "Because that would really make me *really* unhappy. Now, I have been on the road for three days, and I think I've spent about thirty hours in airports. I can't remember the last full night of sleep I had. So it's possible I'm a bit grumpy."

Brit rose from his office chair. He extended his hand and poured all the calming warmth he had into a smile. "We haven't even been properly introduced. Tori, right? Tori Anderson?"

Tori was small—she would tuck nicely against his side, Brit couldn't help but notice—and her face had a hint of pixie about it, heart-shaped, framed by wavy caramel-colored hair that threatened to escape a snug knot at the nape of her neck. But her presence was larger than her frame. If his research hadn't already told him that she was a tough, smart lawyer, the confidence she exuded would have. Behind her hovered one of his lawyers, the ineffectual Harold Tweedy, who couldn't have slowed this woman down if he had thrown his arthritic body to the ground in front of her. She would have simply stepped over him and kept walking.

Though on the other hand... Brit examined her snug black skirt, which outlined a tiny waist and set of nicely rounded hips before ending a few inches above the top of a pair of tall black leather boots. The skirt did look a bit constricting. Perhaps she couldn't step over Harold after all.

"Tori, yes, that's me. I've been working with Mr. Tweedy over here for weeks. I thought I was coming here to put the finishing touches on our deal. Now, he says you need to meet with me personally. He says you told him to restructure this contract, including terms we eliminated weeks ago." She stepped closer, ignoring his outstretched hand. "I want to work with you, Mr. Bencher. I really do. But I don't play games, and I'm not going to waste my client's time and money."

He motioned toward a small conference table, tucked into a corner of his office. "I don't want to waste anyone's time, least of all your client's. Why don't you sit down and we can talk?" He waited until her back was to him before shooting Harold a "get the hell out of my office and don't come back" look. The balding man's eyes widened, and he backed up so quickly he almost tripped over his own feet.

Brit had tried being nice to Harold. He'd tried shooing him gently out of the room when he needed a break from the older man's habit of slowing down every transaction with excessive lawyering. Eventually, Brit had discovered that the only thing to do was order him to leave. Firmly. And then accept his naysaying and disaster-scenario-spinning on the other end.

"I guess I'll be going then," Harold said from the hall. "Nice to see you, Tori."

"You too, Harold," she called back.

Brit closed the door behind Harold and turned to Tori. He finally had her alone.

Now, the fun began.

• • •

Tori's eyes narrowed in suspicion. Why would a hotshot CEO step into an already negotiated contract to offer *better* terms at the last minute? He certainly didn't *look* guilty, but Tori's legal instincts were kicking into high gear. Something was up. She'd bet her upcoming partnership seat on it.

Tori's Rules of Negotiation Number One: beware of sexy CEOs bearing favorable contracts.

Sure, his thick black hair, olive skin, and crystal blue eyes made him look like sex-on-a-stick. Fine. She didn't swoon. It wasn't in her nature. She could handle his tall-dark-and-gorgeous six-foot-tall frame, and the fact that he'd somehow earned the god-awful nickname of The Slayer for his effect on women. She wasn't a teenager, after all.

What she *couldn't* shake was him coming in at the last minute of a deal she'd been working on for months and offering what seemed to be terms too good to be true. That was unacceptable.

She settled into a wooden chair that probably cost him a thousand dollars. She forced herself to keep hold of her temper, while a litany of nasty insults flew through her mind. "Now, Mr. Bencher, I must note that you asked your lawyer to leave us. Are you sure you want to negotiate without the benefit of an attorney?"

He smiled through a set of perfect white teeth. "Call me Brit."

Tori reciprocated with a smile so sweet it curdled her stomach. "Brit."

"And I'll call you Tori."

Oh dear God, what was this? He was gazing directly into her eyes, and for the first time it occurred to her that he sounded as if he might be…could he be…flirting?

"Okaaay," she said slowly. Her heart gave an

uncomfortable thump. Even though she didn't trust his inviting gaze for a moment, she wasn't entirely immune to his hundred-million-dollar charm."

You are aware that it is customary to use attorneys when negotiating a deal of this magnitude, right?" Tori asked, if only to distract herself from the burning sensation that had begun somewhere around the pit of her stomach.

Brit waved a hand. "Oh, I'll get Harold back in here eventually. He'll wet his pants if I leave him outside too long."

She darted a look at the door. "Wait, you mean he's still out there?"

"Probably."

She stared, astonished. "Your lawyer stands outside your door and waits for you?"

"My lawyer drives me crazy. I have to make him wait around outside or he starts to assume I'll listen to his advice. This way, I keep him on his toes."

Tori blinked. "That is the oddest attorney-client relationship I have ever heard of."

Brit waved. "He's been working for Excorp for thirty years. He's like a fixture here. There's no way I can fire him, but there's also no way I'll let him beat a deal to death."

Now they were getting into it. Tori narrowed her gaze. "Was he beating the deal to death? I had the impression we were negotiating."

"You were stuck," Brit said. "He wanted to impose conditions on you that you'd never accept. You wanted more money than we'd ever give."

"And your point is?"

"I asked him to make a few changes in the contract."

Tori cleared her throat. "I noticed."

"You don't like it," he concluded.

"I think that's safe to say. Yes, we were at a bit of a tough spot, but we could have reached an agreement. Now…" She shook her head and tapped the paper in front of her. "You made significant changes to the deal. I don't like surprises, Mr. Bencher, and this was a big surprise."

"Brit," he reminded her. "And you'll like it. The changes aren't as dramatic as they seem. I told Harold to add back an indemnity provision but include a few exceptions for your client's financial protection, and offered a goodwill option to increase the purchase price. I think you'll appreciate what I've done."

Tori leaned back in her chair. He casually spun a pen between two of his fingers, and she couldn't help but notice that they didn't look like the hands of a businessman. They were too competent. Square and solid. Like he could box a few rounds or fix a leaky roof.

She cleared her throat. "I thought we were at the end of our negotiations. I was ready to make a deal. Now?" She held up her hands. "I don't know."

"You know," Brit said. "You'll come around. You don't like that I moved the finish line, but you can't pretend you don't like the outcome."

"I need to think about it," she forced herself to say pleasantly. "And talk to my client."

"Of course." Brit rose to his feet. He checked his watch. "Still morning. Plenty of time for you to read this over and talk to Mr. Tollefson before we go to dinner."

"Dinner?"

"The meal after lunch? Before breakfast?"

"I know what dinner is." Tori spoke each word carefully. "I don't understand why you want to eat it with me."

His gaze lingered on her face and then trailed across her body. It wasn't so obvious as to be insulting but was enough to send a trail of heat across her skin.

Crap. He *was* flirting with her!

"I'd like to get to know you better," Brit said.

"If you think you can get a better deal out of me by buying me dinner, think again."

Brit waved a hand dismissively. "For heaven's sake, nothing could be further from my mind. You make your decision about the deal first. Then we eat. It's only dinner, Tori."

Tori cringed. Of course it was only dinner. What did she think, The Slayer wanted to have sex with her? The Slayer dated supermodels, heiresses, and size-zero women who *didn't* eat the doughnuts that someone set out in the break room every Monday morning. He did not date women whose idea of a party was leaving the office by eight, instead of ten, at night.

"I'll think about it," she said, uncomfortable over being asked out by a client, much less one as sexy as Brit, and hoped her cheeks weren't as red as they felt. "After I look at the deal."

He wrote down a number on the back of a business card. "That's my cell phone. Call me when you're ready."

Chapter Two

"Hey, Tori! Am I a millionaire yet?"

The exuberant voice of Jerry Tollefson, president and founder of Technix, boomed through the phone. Tori winced. She'd spent four hours combing through the contract and reviewing case law and had even asked one of the senior partners, Ellis Heatherington, to review the changes. Finally, she had to admit that the deal was a good one. As fun as it would have been, she simply couldn't justify rejecting the deal simply to make a point with Brit Bencher.

Ellis, whose idea of positive feedback generally amounted to, "Glad you didn't screw this one up, Anderson," had been practically effusive on the phone.

"Lock it down. You won't do better for your client." Ellis *had paused, as if he could barely force the words from his mouth.* "And congratulations. I'll make sure the partnership committee hears about this."

"Hold on, Jerry. There have been some changes to their offer. That's why I'm calling." She took a deep breath. Even with the senior partner's praise ringing in her ears, Tori still hated to deliver the news to Jerry. Not because it was bad or even because Jerry would care—she knew he wouldn't—but because, in a sense, it meant the other side had won.

Something was just off with Brit Bencher stepping in at the last minute like this. Tori couldn't put her finger on it, so she hesitated to mention her misgivings to Jerry.

"They still want to buy the company?"

"Yes."

"Then what's the holdup?"

Tori gritted her teeth. Jerry was the most brilliant software designer she had ever met, but he had no head for legal details. "They want indemnity."

"I thought you said we weren't going to agree to that."

"I did, but things have changed." She explained the new contract provisions Brit had added, and described the way he'd structured the indemnity so that Jerry wasn't at risk the way he might have been otherwise.

"Lord, Tori, I don't care about any of this. What do you think?"

"They've increased the purchase price by five million." Her mouth suddenly went dry. She swallowed hard and forced herself spit out the words. "I think you should take it."

Jerry whistled low. "That's a lot of trips to Boca. Listen, you know I trust you. If you're okay with it, I'm okay with it."

Tori sighed. Though she appreciated the sentiment, she didn't like having her clients make uninformed decisions. "Ellis read it over as well. He recommended you accept."

"Sounds great to me." Jerry started to whistle the theme from *Hawaii Five-O*.

Tori smiled, but a nagging feeling in her chest forced her to continue, and she wanted to kick herself for actually being excited about a possible date with Brit. "There's something else…" It felt odd to bring it up, but Tori had to admit she was dying to tell someone what had happened in Brit's office.

That, and on the off-chance that it did turn into a real date, she wanted Jerry's consent before she went any further.

"What?"

"Brit Bencher wants to take me out to dinner."

Jerry sucked in a breath. "The Slayer? Wow, you didn't think he'd even show up for the meeting. So, have dinner. Maybe you can get me a couple extra million if you bat those pretty eyelashes of yours at him."

"Jerry, can you be serious for a minute?" Tori jumped up from the hotel bed and began to pace the room. "I'm sure it's nothing, but we *are* on opposite sides of this deal. I don't want you to think I'd compromise your position."

The humor fell away from Jerry's voice. "Look, ever since I first came to you for help, you've done everything humanly possible for me, and don't think I don't know it. I wouldn't worry for a minute that you'd let anything get between you and the deal. You never have and you never will."

"But—"

"Do you want me to tell you not to go?"

She paused. *Was* that what she wanted? "No, I'm confused." She wandered into the bathroom and stared at herself in the mirror. The harsh fluorescent lights made her skin look yellow, and the bags under her eyes glowed like twin bruises. Yeah, there was definitely something up with The Slayer asking *this* out on a date.

"I can't imagine what he wants with me."

There was silence, then a low chuckle. "Tori, you don't need me to explain the birds and the bees, do you? I seem to recall Phil wasn't much of a man, but he did know how to... er..."

"Jerry!" She couldn't help but laugh. Jerry had never thought much of her ex-fiancé, and truth be told, neither had Tori. But Phil had seemed so steady. So predictable.

The kind of guy who would never leave his wife and

daughter to become a scuba instructor in Hawaii.

Tori shook the sudden image of her father from her mind. "Look, I'm about five years older, eight inches shorter, and twenty pounds heavier than the type he's usually seen with. I'm sure it's not a date. He's probably being polite."

"Tori." He heaved a loud sigh. "My dear, you have no idea how attractive you are. I know a dozen men who would kill to take you out, but you refuse every time I bring them up. When's the last time you went on a date, anyway?"

She closed the toilet and sat on the lid, refusing to look again at the woman in the mirror. "A few months?"

"Try nine. You brought Richard Finnley to my Technix party. He's an accountant, for God's sake."

"What's wrong with accountants?"

"Nothing, if they're real men. Richard Finnley does not qualify as a real man."

Richard was exactly Tori's height, a sweet man with soft hands and a sharp mind. Unfortunately, Jerry was right. By the end of the night, it had become clear that he was more interested in handling Tori's finances than handling her.

"Still...The Slayer? What would I do with him?"

"If you're asking me that question, then you really need this. Go have fun, Tori. Have sex with a hot guy. Live in the moment."

"Jerry!" Tori's eyes felt like they were going to pop out of her head. "I couldn't!"

"Maybe you should."

"We're negotiating a deal, Jerry."

"You told me that the deal is done," Jerry pointed out. "You told me to accept the offer. I've accepted."

"The contract isn't final," Tori muttered.

"If you're really worried about it, ask Ellis to review it again before I sign. I don't care. Seriously, I've been worried about you lately. You're working too hard. You don't seem happy."

She moistened the end of her finger and rubbed at a water spot on her boot. "I know I've been tense lately but I can't slack off now. They've been ruthless with the associates the past couple of years. If I want to make partner, I've got to have amazing numbers, and I missed all that work last year when my mom had pneumonia—"

Jerry snorted. "You bill twice the hours of the other slackers at that firm and you know it. But I'm not going to give you a hard time about it now. I want you to have some fun. I know you've got a thing against good-looking men, but try to put it aside. We're not all bad."

Though Tori sometimes forgot because she had been friends with Jerry so long, he was a ladies' man in his own right, with longish blond hair and a tall, rangy build. Perhaps it was the fact that he was a client, or perhaps the chemistry simply wasn't there, but in either case, Tori never thought of Jerry as anything other than a brilliant software designer and dear friend.

"Don't worry, Jerry," she said. "I don't consider you one of them."

"You're lying. But I forgive you." The laughter slowly left his voice. "You know, you're also one of the few people in this world I care about, so you tell him you've got a much stronger, better-looking guy on your side, if he doesn't play nice."

Tori snorted. "Right. I'll make sure to do that first thing. Thanks for the date, Mr. Bencher, but I want you to know if you aren't nice to me, my friend Jerry will beat you up."

Jerry paused. Tori realized what she'd said a moment too late to recall the words. She could practically hear one of Jerry's bushy blond eyebrows raise in his trademark ironic gesture.

"But Tori," he said, his voice laced with wicked amusement, "I thought this wasn't a date."

. . .

After finishing her call with Jerry, Tori lay down on the bed and stared at the ceiling. She thought about Fritzy, and Mrs. Jenkins.

Maybe she was working too hard. Maybe she did need to let loose, take her mind off work for a night.

The very thought of letting loose with Brit Bencher sent a rush of heat from her cheeks to the tips of her toes. With a sigh of pure desire, she let herself play out the fantasy. Imagined his strong hands slipping off her coat, caressing her through her thin silk blouse, and then pulling up her skirt and sliding over her hips to the warm, wet place in between.

A buzz from her BlackBerry shook Tori from her erotic reverie. With a deep sigh, she sat up and scrolled through her in-box. Twenty unread messages, most from Karl Bulcher, her most demanding client. They had a 9:00 a.m. meeting the day after tomorrow, and he wanted to move it to seven. Seven in the *morning*.

She'd be exhausted. Jet-lagged. In desperate need of a day off. And thanks to Karl she'd now be going into the office at 7:00 a.m.

Work. That was her life. Not hot sex with guys like The Slayer.

Anyway, Brit had asked her to dinner, not a naked hot tub party. He was being polite. Either that, or he wanted something from her and it had nothing to do with sex.

Tori's Rules of Negotiation Number Two: assume nothing. If he came on to her, well, she would have to cross that bridge when she came to it. But she wouldn't hold her breath waiting, and she refused to play the fool. She'd learned that from her mother.

No man would get the better of Tori Anderson. Even if he was The Slayer.

Chapter Three

Tori smoothed her hair and peered into the mirror for the hundredth time as she waited for the soft buzz of the hotel phone. After reluctantly calling Brit and agreeing both to the basic terms of the deal and to dinner, she had taken a long soak in the hotel's hot tub and an equally long shower. In that time, she had gathered any number of reasons to call him back and cancel their date.

For one, Brit was far too charming. Tori had never trusted charming men—they reminded her of her father. That was why she preferred to date men like Phil and Richard Finnley. They were smart, decent men, without a charming bone in their bodies.

What if Brit did want something more than just dinner? Like a kiss, maybe? She tried to imagine him leaning in toward her and burst out laughing. Next thing she knew, she'd be imagining flying unicorns and sparkly fairies taking her for a ride on a rainbow.

Tori grabbed her boots from the tiny hotel closet, sat down on the edge of the bed, and then began the arduous process of shoving her extra-wide feet through the extra-narrow leather.

A soft knock startled her from her reverie. She hopped awkwardly toward the door, still shoving her right foot into her boot. Stumbling over her own feet, Tori barely caught the door handle before awkwardly regaining her balance. She opened the door.

The sultry fragrance of lilies tickled her nose. She stared in shock at a bouquet of white and pink Stargazers, then let her gaze travel slowly up the outstretched arm of the man offering them to her.

"Brit?" she breathed with horror. He was early. Not to mention standing in the hall outside her door instead of meeting her in the lobby like she'd expected. "What are you doing here?"

She tried not to picture the room behind her. She had only been there for a night, but after years of traveling, she tended to treat hotel rooms like second homes. The unfortunate unpadded bra had been flung across an end table, and her black lace nightgown lay on the armchair by the bed. Her laptop was blinking on the desk, a mountain of paperwork beside it, and the remnants of her half-starved raid on the minibar—M&M's wrappers, a can of Diet Pepsi, and a half-empty bag of peanuts—littered the other available surfaces.

He chuckled. "If I didn't know better, I'd say you aren't happy to see me."

Though she wouldn't have thought it possible, he looked even better now than he had in the Excorp boardroom. His pinstriped suit and power tie had been replaced by a pair of snug-fitting khakis and a midnight blue sweater. Broad shoulders simply begged to be touched, and his narrow waist gave her visions of running her fingers along the inside of his pants.

A rush of adrenaline jump-started her heart into a

staccato rhythm.

She swallowed hard. "I thought you were going to meet me in the lobby."

He shrugged. "I changed my mind."

Changed his mind? Brit Bencher didn't change his mind. He had come up here for a reason. Her eyes narrowed. If this were a negotiation, she'd say he was trying to throw her off her guard, fluster her by showing up at her door. But to what end? A man like Brit didn't have to play games to get a woman in his bed.

She studied him a moment, then shook her head. No sense trying to read his mind. She would know soon enough what he wanted. Meanwhile, Tori's Rules of Negotiation Number Three: when in doubt, attack.

Forcing a wide, easy smile, she took the flowers and pulled open the door. "Come in."

Tori set the bouquet on the desk, picked up her nightgown, and threw it into her open suitcase. Her heart leapfrogged from *rapid* to *I just ran a marathon and think I might die.*

What was she doing? Playing games with The Slayer?

Had she lost her mind?

Brit's broad-shouldered frame easily filled the small space between the single queen-size bed and wooden wardrobe. A smile hovered around the corners of his mouth. "No need to tidy up on my account. I really ought to have called first."

If anything, he seemed to grow more comfortable the longer he was in her room. Absurd to think a woman's negligee could make The Slayer nervous.

Tori knew she had lost control of the situation—no, scratch that: she'd never *had* control. She'd been insane to think she could hold her own against a man like Brit.

Her mind spun furiously. Should she retreat? Swear off dinner?

No. Her pride screamed in protest. *No way.*

She found herself staring at his lips as a fresh wave of panic passed over her.

She thought about Jerry, nine months without a date, and gritted her teeth.

There would be no retreat.

"I made us a reservation at Alessandro's," Brit continued, unaware of the battle raging inside Tori's mind. "It's a little Italian place in Queens. You aren't one of those low-carb fanatics, are you?"

Tori had told him to pick the spot for dinner, curious to see what his selection of restaurant would reveal. "Pasta is one of the reasons I get out of bed in the morning. That, and a nice piece of white toast with a slab of butter for breakfast."

The words were a form of challenge. *Go ahead*, she thought, *compare me to your model girlfriends. Be my guest.*

His smile widened. "I like where you're headed. Now add a couple of fried eggs and some real hash browns and you're in business."

"Real hash browns, huh?" She crossed her arms below her breasts, forcing the soft fabric of her dress to stretch tightly over her full C-cups.

"Shredded or cubed?"

"Shredded, naturally."

She allowed herself a smile. "Now there's a man who knows how to eat. We'll get along fine, Mr. Bencher."

"Brit," he reminded her.

"Where did you come up with Brit?" she asked. "Isn't your real name John?"

"You've been reading about me?" He lifted one eyebrow and leaned against the wardrobe, thrusting one hand casually into his pant pocket. The move made the fabric pull tighter across his groin.

Tori's pulse skipped a beat. "Research. Know thy opponent, and all that jazz."

"Well, if I tell you how I got my name, you'll have to tell me why you turned down a clerkship with a Supreme Court justice."

She sucked in a breath. "How in the world did you find that out?"

"Research."

No one knew about the clerkship offer. Not even her mother—or rather, *especially* her mother, who was the reason she had been forced to turn it down. Whatever modicum of control Tori thought she had managed to retain slipped through her fingers.

"Why don't we head down to dinner?" She had no intention of discussing her clerkship, or any other matter involving her mother, with Brit Bencher.

His steely gaze assessed, analyzed, and then silently agreed to back off. He glanced at her thin jersey dress with its deep V-neck. "It's a bit chilly. Do you have a coat?"

She shook her head. "I try to travel light."

"I'll have the car brought around." He pulled a cell phone from his pocket and stepped back toward the door to the room, speaking quietly.

Tori took advantage of his distraction to scroll quickly through the messages on her BlackBerry. Her fingers trembled; she needed the familiar sight of the mountain of work waiting for her to break through her panic.

At least at work she knew what she should do. Unlike here, in this hotel room, where she was completely lost.

Brit finished his brief call and slipped his phone into his pocket. Tori fumbled with her purse, throwing in her hotel key card and wallet, noting as she did that her secret condom stash still had at least one foil-wrapped packet in it.

Oh dear God, what if he did *want to have sex? Could she do it?*

When she looked up again her face was burning. If

only Brit didn't have that tiny bend to his nose, the one that suggested he'd broken it in his youth, then perhaps she might not be acting like a hormone-driven teenager. But his combination of tough and sexy was giving her hives.

She cleared her throat. "I guess I'm ready."

He surveyed her from head to toe. "Are you sure you're a lawyer?"

Suddenly aware of the curve of her waist and the way the dress outlined her thighs, Tori felt a rush of pure feminine pleasure. Finally, something she could say for certain: Brit hadn't invited her out to dinner to talk business. Brit was coming on to her.

But why?

And did it matter?

He's on the other side of the deal, her sensible lawyer-self said.

You finished negotiating the deal this afternoon, her sex-starved-self retorted. *Besides, your client gave you permission. Hell, he suggested it!*

She forced her mind back to the present. "As hard as it may be to believe, there are actually a number of female attorneys in the business world these days."

He placed one hand at the small of her back. "I heard a rumor to that effect."

Tori wet her lips.

Blue eyes threatened to swallow her whole. "Let's test, shall we? To make sure you're real."

Her body froze, taut as a violin string, practically vibrating with the force of his magnetic pull.

Deliberately, he moved his hand from her back to her waist. A thumb brushed the soft, sensitive skin of her stomach. Her mouth parted in anticipation, and then it was captured by his warm, seeking lips.

Chapter Four

Tori's hand instinctively rose to clutch Brit's shoulder. It was hard and muscled, exactly the way she had envisioned. His lips were firm, expert. He claimed her mouth in a single breath. A shudder went through her and the tingle that had begun the moment he walked in the room turned into a full-bodied ache.

She moved her mouth against his, and his tongue penetrated her parted lips. Heat suffused her body as she pressed against him, opening her mouth and giving him room to play. Their tongues meshed, a delicate dance of exploration and wanting. Her body melted into his, hips, breasts, and legs all seeking further contact. As the kiss deepened, Tori's knees began to tremble.

Then, inexplicably, he pulled back.

Brit touched her face with one large hand and then placed it at the top of her hip. They stood suspended, bodies touching, chests moving in rapid rhythm.

"If we don't go to dinner now, I'm not going to let you out of this room."

Flushed with pleasure, Tori dropped her eyes and reluctantly released the arms that had wound tightly around his neck. "I bet you say that to all the women who are negotiating million-dollar agreements with you."

She started to move away, struggling to regain her equanimity, but Brit stopped her, his hand tightening around her waist.

"Let's make a deal," he said. "You don't mention Technix for the rest of the night, and I'll do the same."

"Why?" She cursed the slow reaction of her brain, still fogged with pleasure. Their bodies were too close; too close to think, too close to breathe.

"Why? Because that's not what tonight's about." He drew back, as if insulted by her question.

Tori shook her head. "Look, I don't normally go around having romantic encounters with the guy on the other side of a deal. I suppose I'd like to know why you're doing this. It doesn't seem like such an odd thing to ask."

"It's quite simple," he said, gazing intently down at her. "I want you."

Tori sucked in a breath as his casual pronouncement. She'd never been the subject of such blatant male intent. Her palms began to sweat.

"And what makes you so sure I'm interested?"

He ran a hand along the side of her waist, skimming her rib cage and almost, but not quite, touching the underside of her breast.

"Call it instinct. My car is waiting outside. We don't want to be late for our reservation."

· · ·

They stopped in front of the elevators, the air thick with tension. When the doors opened with a muted *ding*, Brit gestured for Tori to go first. As the doors closed behind them, she imagined Brit throwing her against the back wall, pulling her dress to her waist and taking her, right then and there. Warmth pooled between her legs. By the time they reached the ground floor, Tori could feel the tickle of sweat between her shoulder blades.

Nothing in her life had prepared her for this moment. Panic and excitement mixed in equal parts. Clearly, she had stepped inside some *other* woman's life. Some woman who had crazy one-night stands with gorgeous CEOs.

Please, woman whose life I stole—can I keep it? For one night?

After threading their way through the crowded lobby and a revolving door to the street beyond, Brit guided her past a line of waiting taxicabs to a sleek black Mercedes with dark tinted windows. A driver in a black suit nodded as he held open a door for Tori. The air had a rare bite for late June, and she gratefully slipped inside to a warm leather seat. Brit followed closely behind, and when he sat down, their legs touched from hip to thigh.

She scooted to the side, needing a moment without his touch to clear her head. This relentless onslaught of sensuality had her head spinning. Either he was one of the best liars she'd ever met or he meant what he said.

I want you.

The very thought of those words, spoken so casually, sent a flare of heat through her body.

He wanted her.

Brit Bencher wanted her, Tori Anderson. A short, curvy, attorney who didn't have a supermodel bone in her body. It was too much to be believed.

The car was open between the front and the back, and when the driver sat down, relief flooded through her. Being alone with Brit right now was more than she could handle.

"Have you spent much time in New York?" Brit asked, his deep voice filling the small space.

"I assumed your spies already revealed that information."

He chuckled. "Humor me. I can't remember everything they said."

"I went to Yale Law and did a summer internship at a firm in town. So I know Manhattan, at least. But that was only for one summer. I come up for business fairly regularly, but that rarely gets me far from my hotel."

"Well, we're headed for Queens. Alessandro's serves simple, rich, Italian fare. Nothing fancy, but an Alfredo sauce like none other. Unless you'd prefer something more upscale tonight? L'Atelier? If you feel like sushi there's always Masa."

Tori shook her head. She knew both restaurants, and their prices were astronomical. The last thing she wanted was to feel indebted to Brit. "No. Simple sounds perfect. I've been on the road for the past week and haven't seen a decent plate of pasta in far too long. I love seeing my clients, but I must admit, the traveling gets to me."

"So you were doing client visits this week?"

"Yes, and I really can't complain. The partners know I'll do anything for a new client, so when they get leads that look like a long shot, they give them to me. I flew from Philly to Texas, and then to Florida to meet with a potential client who wants to build a resort in the Keys."

"So you've got clients doing everything from real estate to robotics?"

She pushed a strand of hair back behind her ear and ignored the attempt at humor. Suspicion prickled along her spine, as it did whenever anyone mentioned her most famous—and secretive—client. "Your spies told you about Solen Labs?"

"It was hardly a secret," he said dryly. "You made quite a name for yourself when you helped them break away from

MIT."

She studied his face, looking for any hint that his choice of topic was more than polite conversation, but saw nothing. The signs, billboards, and headlights of passing cars flickered across an impassive face. She was about to quiz him further, but his gaze dropped to her mouth, and she had to fight the urge to lean in for another kiss.

"I knew Garth Solen from high school," she said. "He helped me get through algebra. He approached me not long after I started practicing law. He'd been forced to turn down an investor because they didn't meet university criteria, and decided it was time to take the lab private."

"Is it true that no one at the lab actually knows where he lives, or what his cell number is?"

She smiled. "Not really. But Garth is a very private man. Those of us who work closely with him understand the ground rules. Respect that privacy, or he's outta there."

Brit's finger brushed the inside of her knee. In the uneven glow the planes of his cheekbones were defined by dark shadows. Her throat momentarily swelled shut.

"You have an advantage over me," she managed to choke out. "I don't have spies. I don't know anything about you."

That wasn't precisely true. She *had* studied his profile before the meeting. But it was public information, nothing nearly as personal as her Supreme Court clerkship, or even her work with Solen Labs. Brit Bencher had assumed control of Excorp at the tender age of twenty-five, fresh out of business school. He had taken a small, failing corporation and turned it around. Ten years later Excorp was a giant, publicly traded enterprise with offices in five countries on three continents. And Brit had become legend for his hard-driving, soft-spoken style.

"What would you like to know?"

It was a reasonable question, but his hand had landed on

her knee and she was suddenly having a hard time putting together complete sentences. "I don't…I mean…"

He reached over and touched her cheek. The tip of his thumb brushed across her lips. "We only have a few minutes before we pull up to the restaurant. I should probably save my life story for dinner, don't you think?"

His thumb was turning her brain to Jell-O. She pulled his hand from her face and took a deep breath. "Why don't you start by telling me why you picked this restaurant?"

His teeth glowed in the dark interior of the car. "Okay, if you're determined to do some talking, how about this? I tell you about the restaurant, you let me kiss you again."

He settled his hand around hers. The warmth of it traveled down the length of her arm to her stomach, where it caused a smoldering ember of desire to burst into flame.

"Deal." Anything to get him to stop touching her long enough to regain her wits.

"I used to live in this neighborhood," he began. "When I was young, we didn't have much money, and we only went out to eat once a year—for my mother's birthday. Alessandro's was her favorite. So now I celebrate here when I settle a deal." He traced a lazy circle on the back of her hand. "My turn." He inclined his head and covered her lips in a soft, feather-like kiss.

She froze, almost panicked by the powerful response of her body. Gently, his mouth moved across hers, then slid down the side of her neck. His delicate touch left a waterfall of sensation along her skin. He moved up to the hollow behind her ear, and then nipped gently at her earlobe.

His hand cupped the side of her face, holding her as he returned to her lips and deepened the kiss. They meshed perfectly, exploring mouths and tongues with increasing intensity. Tori arched her back, her breasts aching, needing more contact, more pressure. But he did not touch her anywhere else. Only his mouth ravaged hers, leaving her utterly defenseless. When he sucked gently on her tongue, she dug her nails into the soft leather seat and restrained the urge to drag his body against hers.

Dimly, she felt the car slow, then stop. Brit placed one last kiss on her bruised, tender lips, and smoothed a curl back behind her ear. "Thank you," he murmured, "for the appetizer."

• • •

Brit waited in the car while his driver opened the door and helped Tori out. It had taken all of his will to keep his voice soft and controlled. His entire body ached with frustration. One kiss, one incredible kiss, had gotten him so hard he had seriously considered flipping up the hem of her soft skirt and taking her right there, in the back seat of his car.

This was not how the evening was supposed to go. He was not supposed to be reacting to her like this. He should be cool and controlled, sailing past her defenses with his charm and wit while remaining focused on the prize—Solen's number. But nothing had gone as expected. Her defensiveness and suspicion forced him to kiss her well before he had planned, and instead of disarming her, he'd been the one dizzy and incoherent, forced to pull away before he lost control. And now he was teetering on the edge of insanity, wanting nothing more than to forget about Solen, take Tori home, and make love to her all night long.

To make matters worse, he was already feeling guilty about misleading her about the reason for dinner. For all her toughness, when he kissed her at the hotel he'd seen a vulnerability in Tori's eyes that hit him like a punch to the gut. The thought of abusing that innocence left him sick.

Remember Melissa, he told himself. *This is about Melissa.*

He forced himself to jump out and lead Tori into the restaurant. Her skin was flushed and rosy, her full lips slightly parted. She had a bemused, almost glassy look to her eyes that made him want to kiss her insensible all over again.

He'd discovered Tori's name while researching Solen. People said she was young, driven, and Solen's primary link to the outer world. She also happened to be negotiating a deal with his company. For once, Brit thought, his silly reputation with women would come in handy. He'd take her out to dinner, turn on a little charm, and feed her Melissa's story. She'd be sympathetic—what woman wouldn't be?—and hand over the number before dessert. He'd even sweetened the deal for her client.

He had never imagined that *he* might be the one losing control.

A young, dark-haired waitress in a low-necked peasant blouse greeted them by the crowded front entry. "Welcome to Alessandro's," she said, reserving a warm smile for Brit.

"Serena, how are you?" He leaned forward and kissed both her cheeks.

She flushed prettily. "I'd be better if you came by more often. Follow me, your table is ready."

The restaurant was exactly as he had described it—a cheerful place made for families, birthdays, and celebrations. There were red-and-white checked tablecloths, white carnations next to flickering tea lights, and comfortable round-backed armchairs. The air was heavy with the smells of garlic and oregano, saffron and espresso. A bar at the back of the room was packed with a crowd ranging from couples in their twenties to older men, all laughing loudly and drinking.

Tori practically flinched at the jealous looks of the dozen or so people waiting by the front door. Her features displayed every turn of her emotions, from hot passion to nervous tension. "I suppose you know someone?" she asked.

"Frank Alessandro, the owner. He's a good friend of the family."

Serena led them through an arched doorway into a second, quieter room and pointed them toward a small table in the back corner. Brit held out the chair for Tori and pushed it in behind her. For a second, he allowed his hand to brush against her neck, and smiled with satisfaction when she shivered in response.

Once they were seated, the waitress handed out menus, giving Brit a wink as she did. "I would tell you about the specials, but Frank finished a fresh batch of your Alfredo sauce a few minutes ago. I think you had better order it."

"I wouldn't dream of doing anything else." Brit ignored the menu. "Can you bring us a bottle of red to start? Whatever Frank recommends."

"Absolutely." She nodded and headed back for the front.

"I like this place," Tori said with surprise. "It's definitely not what I expected."

"What did you expect?"

"Something a bit flashier, to be honest."

"Flashy? Where would you get that idea?"

She grinned. "I don't know, let's see…you're the CEO of a large, successful company, your nickname is The Slayer, and weren't they going to make a reality show about you? *The Bachelor NYC*?"

He chuckled. "Don't believe everything you read. But you're right. I don't bring many people here. It's really more of a family place."

"So why did you bring me?" Her eyes gleamed with suspicion.

Careful, Brit. She's too damn smart to fall for a line.

"Honestly, I'm not sure. I had a feeling you'd enjoy it." He shrugged at the unintended confession, and watched her tongue flick over her bottom lip. He let his gaze linger there, then sweep over her full breasts.

"Tell me about your family," she said, her words tripping over each other in her eagerness to change the subject. He noted with satisfaction that she flushed under his regard. "You're the eldest?"

"Yes, lucky me." Out of the corner of his eye, Brit noticed a familiar stocky figure enter the room. He looked away quickly, hoping to escape notice, but it was no use. He tried not to glower too obviously. "Believe it or not, here comes one of my brothers now."

"Hey, ugly, long time no see!" Ross called out, his eyes darting instantly to Tori.

Brit stood and gave Ross the back-pounding that was their traditional greeting. His younger brother by only thirteen months, Ross was broader in the chest, more heavily muscled than Brit, and spent time keeping it that way. They shared the same olive skin as their mother and square jaw of their father, but otherwise could not have been more different. In school, Ross enjoyed the rough camaraderie of football, while Brit preferred the solitary competition of track. Ross was a builder, always working with his hands, while Brit spent much of their childhood with his nose buried in a book.

Ross beamed down at Tori. "Well, well, well, who do we have here?"

Brit's felt his smile grow tight. The other thing he and Ross shared was an intense sibling rivalry that had often manifested itself in a competition over women. He stepped back and gestured reluctantly toward Tori. "Tori Anderson, this is my brother Ross Bencher. Ross, this is Tori. She and I are working on a deal together."

"Pleased to meet you," Tori said.

Ross pressed a kiss to the back of Tori's hand and gave her a playful leer. "The pleasure is all mine."

Brit fought a sudden desire to plant a fist right in the

middle of the six-pack of which his brother was so proud.

As Tori started to stand, Ross released her hand and waved her back to her seat. "Please, don't get up. I don't want to disturb your dinner."

You mean you want to keep eyeing her cleavage.

Brit angled his body in between them. "So, little brother, what brings you in tonight? I thought the kids were with you this week."

Ross held out his hands and shrugged helplessly. "They're at home with Mariel. I couldn't face another one of my meatball sandwiches so I stopped in for some Alfredo. Mariel's my next-door neighbor," he explained to Tori. "I have custody of my kids every other week and she helps out when I've got an emergency. Like tonight."

"You really shouldn't leave them with a neighbor," Brit said with a frown. Sometimes he wondered how Ross's ex-wife could have agreed to shared custody. "Besides, isn't it past bedtime?"

"Brit fancies himself everyone's father," Ross confided to Tori. "He thinks I'm an absolutely hopeless parent."

"Oh really?" She gave Ross one of her warm, genuine smiles. "That's hard to believe."

"All too true," Ross said, warming to his topic. "And you wouldn't believe the way he hovers over our sister, Melissa. It's a wonder she doesn't—"

"Don't you need to check on your order?" Brit asked. The last thing he needed was for Ross to open his big mouth.

"No, Serena's bringing it out to me." Ross glanced back and forth between Tori and Brit, his gaze turning speculative. "So what brings you to Alessandro's, big brother? This isn't your usual after-work hangout."

"I thought Tori would enjoy Frank's Alfredo."

"Is that right?" Ross waited for a moment.

Brit tightened his jaw and refused to elaborate.

Damned if he was going to explain anything to his distinctly untrustworthy brother.

"I'm flying back to Philly tomorrow," Tori added. "I'm only in town for the night."

"You know, it's interesting. I don't think Brit's ever brought anyone here before. At least, not that I've ever seen."

Serena appeared with a brown paper bag and handed it to Ross. He took it and gave her a kiss on the cheek. "Looks like I'm ready to go. You two have a nice dinner. Brit, I'll see you next Saturday. Don't forget, Luke has a game at eleven."

Brit snorted. "You've forgotten more games than I have." He sighed with relief as Ross said good-bye to Tori and left the room. "Sometimes it's great to have a close family, and sometimes…"

Tori glanced at Ross's retreating back. "He seems very nice."

Nice like a hyena, Brit thought. "Sometimes I get a little tired of cleaning up after him, but someone's got to do it. What about you?" he asked. "Any brothers or sisters?"

"No. Just me and my mom." She buried her head in her menu. "I suppose I better take a look at my options—or should I go with the Alfredo?"

Brit made a mental note to find out what had happened to the mother she was so uncomfortable talking about.

"Trust me," he said. He pulled the menu from her trembling hands. She was too bright for him to bring up Solen now, he thought, with a small amount of relief. Perhaps after dinner. Yes, that was it. When they'd had a few bottles of wine, and her defenses were down. He'd ask her about Solen then.

"I'll take care of you tonight," Brit promised. "I'll take care of everything."

Chapter Five

After Ross's departure and several glasses of an excellent merlot, Tori began to relax enough to enjoy Brit's company. He kept her off-balance by alternatively stroking her hand and gently touching her knee under the table, but she managed not do anything morbidly embarrassing, like drop a noodle down her dress, spill her wine, or say anything further about her mother.

It took some effort, though, to silence her mother's voice, echoing in her mind.

He's not your type, Tori.

Never trust a charming man, Tori.

He'll break your heart, Tori. Men like that always do.

Resolutely, she pushed the familiar warnings aside. Tonight was going to be different. Brit's behavior around his brother, the possessive, almost proprietary way he growled at Ross when he kissed her hand, had finally convinced her that this date might be for real. She convinced herself to relax and enjoy whatever the night may bring.

At least for now. When they were alone, she planned on freaking out all over again.

The Alfredo was indeed something to write home about—creamy and fragrant, and so rich she could eat only a tiny portion of the enormous plate she was served. Brit was as funny and charming as the gossip rags suggested. He made her laugh with his dead-on imitation of Harold, and they discovered a shared love of unhealthy food and good wine. In fact, the evening passed so quickly that Tori was shocked it was after midnight when they finally headed out for Brit's car.

The wine had left her head pleasantly fuzzy, and she leaned gratefully on Brit's arm as he guided her out the restaurant door and into the waiting Mercedes. Ella Fitzgerald's throaty voice filled the interior as Tori leaned her head against the back of the seat and slouched down into the soft leather.

Putting her arms behind her ears, she stretched languidly. "Mmmm," she sighed. "That was truly an exceptional meal. Frank makes the finest tiramisu I've ever tasted." The chef had come to their table not long after they finished the main course. He had insisted she try the rich, espresso-soaked cake, even though Tori protested that she had already gained three pounds from eating her pasta.

Brit cast her an amused look. "You look like a cat, all ready to curl up and take a nap in the sun."

She watched him through her lashes and stretched again. Her body felt heavy and full, the food and the wine combining with a delicious sensual anticipation that left everything clouded in a pleasant haze.

"Meow."

Tori was startled by the sound of her own voice.

Did you actually *make a sound like a cat?*

She was obviously still living some other woman's life. Tori Anderson, workaholic overachiever attorney, would never make that sound. Hell, Tori Anderson would never be here, in the back of a car, with a man destined someday to be voted Sexiest Man in America.

He leaned over and ran a hand along the side of her face, where a mix of waves and curls spilled over her shoulder. In a second, her body became alert, acutely aware of his every move. His fingers stroked the length of her hair, then came back to trace the line of her jaw. Her throat tightened, and without conscious thought, she placed her own hand on his thigh. A muscle moved, hardened under her touch. She slid her hand from his knee to the top of his hip, marveling as she did at the ridges of muscles under her fingers.

They stopped at a red light. As throaty saxophones harmonized with Ella, Brit caught her hand and pulled it to his lips.

"I would take you home with me," he said into her flesh, "but I don't think I can wait that long. Your hotel is closer. Is that all right?"

He waited for a response, leaving the larger question unasked. In a heartbeat, the old Tori Anderson reasserted herself, and her eyes fluttered closed. She didn't even know this man, other than his reputation, and worse yet, they were in the midst of finalizing a deal.

She couldn't. She simply couldn't.

She nodded. "Please."

• • •

By the time they reached the hotel, Tori's entire body was throbbing with a mix of fear and anticipation. Brit led her inside. Though it was late, the lobby was still humming with life, businessmen in suits checking in with black rolling suitcases, women in evening gowns and diamonds laughing from barstools in the restaurant.

The panic that had been toying with her all night returned in a rush as they made their way toward the elevators. She slowed her pace, unable to face what came next.

I shouldn't do this. I can't do this…

Brit stopped. He scrutinized her face, then pulled her into a sheltered alcove. He touched her hand to his lips, breathing gently on it. "Tori, I think you know how I want this evening to end. But if you'd rather I went home now, say so. I won't push you into anything you don't want to do."

"I…I…" She stumbled over the words. Perhaps other, more sophisticated women would know how to act right now, but the truth was, she didn't know the first thing about one-night stands. Especially with men like Brit.

Lord, I can't even get a fling right.

"Tori?"

Damn it!

She tipped her face toward his and heaved a sigh. "I'm sorry, Brit, but I think you should go."

He paused, and in that moment Tori hated herself. She hated her fear, her inability to relax with a beautiful man, and most of all, she hated her total, utter commitment to her job.

"Because of the deal?"

She nodded. "That. And…I can't." She shook her head, wishing she could die, right then and there, and never have to look him in the eye again. "Maybe another time."

Brit touched his hands to her waist. With a smooth, practiced motion, he tugged her closer, until she pressed against the length of him. He barely paused before capturing her mouth, claiming her with a kiss that reached all the way to her toes. When she had been turned from a firm, resolute woman to a helpless creature of need, he pulled back and grinned.

"I'll hold you to that."

Tori sucked in a breath. Dear God, did he *mean* it? The barest hint of an answering smile touched the corner of her mouth.

He placed one final butterfly kiss on the tip of her nose. "Until we meet again."

Then he turned and walked away.

Chapter Six

"You went on a *date* with The Slayer? The SLAYER? I can't believe you waited this long to tell me!"

Betsy's voice started at a whisper but rose with each word. They were standing in the hall in front of Tori's office. Tori checked up and down the sleek, light-filled hallway of the newly remodeled office, her face burning; with her luck a senior partner would pick exactly that moment to wander past. Luckily, the passage was clear. It was almost six-thirty, and most of the lawyers and staff had gone home.

"I don't know what you're talking about," Tori hissed at her assistant. "All I said was that we had dinner. I never said it was a date."

Betsy was a short, round woman with carefully teased black hair that had more than a few streaks of gray, and heavy makeup that she proudly attributed to Avon. Betsy was only forty-five, but she insisted her four children had aged her prematurely. She had been Tori's assistant for four years, ever since Tori joined the firm, and they worked together well, taking turns envying each other's lives. Betsy had a fabulous marriage, great kids, and the air of satisfaction that Tori supposed came from knowing she was doing exactly what she was meant to do. For her part, Betsy envied Tori's travels and her supposedly glamorous, carefree existence.

Betsy wagged a finger at Tori. "I know what you said, but you've been in a daze ever since you walked into the office this afternoon, and I swear I heard you hum. Need I point out that Tori Anderson never hums? You've checked that BlackBerry a hundred times since you got here, and that's bad, even for you. That, and someone delivered three dozen roses to your office while you were in your last meeting."

Tori froze. "Roses?" she croaked. "For me?"

"Yes, you," Betsy laughed. "Don't look so appalled. Roses are a good thing, not a sign of the apocalypse."

Tori was already hurrying into her office, her gaze darting around until she saw the crystal vase filled with dark red roses sitting in the middle of her enormous antique walnut desk, the sultry fragrance already filling the room. Without even pretending not to care, she jerked the envelope from the plastic holder and ripped it open.

Here's to next time—Brit

"Here's to next time?" Betsy shrieked. "Oh my God, did you *sleep* with him?"

Tori spun around. "Betsy, hush!" She jumped up to close the door to her office. "Of course I didn't sleep with him. We, um, kind of made out."

She shouldn't be telling her secretary this. She shouldn't be telling *anyone* this. But the tiny smile she'd been hiding all day burst free, for one tiny moment. She still couldn't believe she'd kissed Brit Bencher. Maybe she had freaked out afterward, and maybe she didn't have the guts to actually consummate the deal, but hell, he hadn't run screaming from her or laughed at her refusal to let him spend the night. What kind of a man did that?

"Made out? What is this, high school?" Betsy grabbed the card and studied it for a moment. "*Here's to next time*? Sounds like someone wants to finish the job."

"Well, that's romantic." Tori rolled her eyes, though the thought of finishing anything with Brit set every nerve in her body on fire.

Especially the ones between her legs.

"Romance schmo-mance. You'll be back to New York to close the Technix deal in a couple of weeks, right? You can jump in bed with him then."

"I'm going there for business, not to sleep with Brit Bencher. You know I don't have time to fool around, Betsy. I promised the business group I'd do a song and dance about my practice for the summer associates starting next week. I'll need your help with a presentation. And then there's—"

"Karl Bulcher," Betsy interrupted. "I saw your e-mail and I moved the appointment on your calendar to seven tomorrow morning."

Tori rubbed her eyes. The mere mention of Karl was enough to wipe away any remaining giddiness over her night with Brit. "If he's serious about this new acquisition we'll have to start assembling a team. We'll need a few associates, all the summer people, and at least one other paralegal to help with the due diligence."

Betsy held up her hand as if to stop the flood of assignments. "I get the picture. Do you need me to come in early?"

"No, we can work on it when you get in." She opened her eyes to the sight of deep crimson velvety petals. Karl Bulcher disappeared from her thoughts and an image of Brit's eyes, locked on hers as he leaned in for a kiss, appeared in its place.

"Was he as good as they say?"

"Betsy!" Tori said in a strangled voice.

A broad smile brought out the dimples in Betsy's plump cheeks. "I thought so. Man, some people have all the luck. Tell me again why you didn't sleep with him?"

Tori sank into the leather chair behind the desk. "You are incorrigible." She steepled her fingers and rested her chin on top, staring down at the Ben Franklin Parkway and the collection of brightly colored flags that lined it. "We're in the middle of the deal. It was too weird. Besides, he's like a movie star or something. I can't imagine he's really interested in me."

"You have a serious self-esteem problem," Betsy said. "I saw this show once on successful women, and it said they've been conditioned to undervalue their worth—"

"Betsy! If I want a talk show dose of therapy, I promise, I will get one. Anyway, I assume, since you make my calendar, you've looked at it? Did you see a lot of free nights in there?"

"That is your choice, not a requirement," Betsy retorted. "You nailed down the Excorp deal yesterday. You *could* take a night off. No one expects to make partner in their sixth year anymore."

Tori thought about her mother, and Langston Estates. She knew Betsy did, too, because her assistant's face softened, and sympathy creased her heavily made-up eyes.

How much time do I have? A year? Two?

"Oh, hon," Betsy shook her head. "I'm sorry. I understand. At least call Brit back. You've got to say thank you for the flowers, don't you?"

"I'll send him an e-mail."

"You're kidding me. You're really going to walk away from the first real man I've seen you with in the past four years?"

"Have you been talking to Jerry?" Tori asked.

Betsy ignored the question, pinning her down with a mother's glare. "I'm not saying you have to date Fabio, but please, at least go for someone in your own class."

"My class is five-six and pasty. Besides, I don't like charming guys. They're shifty. You can't trust them."

"They're not all like your dad," Betsy said.

Tori ignored the reference to her father. She regretted, not for the first time, the fact that Betsy had known her mother before the Alzheimer's. She leaned back and put her hands in her lap. "Betsy, you researched Brit for me—you know he's with a different girl every week. Why in the world would you want me to go after someone who gives new meaning to the phrase 'love 'em and leave 'em'?"

"Maybe it would be different with you. Maybe you'll be the one to tame his wild, cowboy soul."

A smile cracked the corner of her mouth. "Right. I couldn't tame my own cat." She picked up the top piece of paper from the mountain of correspondence Betsy had stacked beside her computer. "I've got enough work to last me until Christmas. You should get home. I'll see you in the morning."

Pursing her lips, Betsy studied Tori's face. "You flew in this morning from New York, and from the look of those bags under your eyes, I'll guess you only got a few hours of sleep last night. Why not knock off now? The work will be here in the morning."

"No can do. Especially now that I know Karl's serious about this acquisition."

"Remind me exactly why you are the only one who can handle this?" Betsy asked. "Last time I looked there were forty other lawyers in this firm, and any one of them would be happy to take on Mr. Bulcher's latest project."

Tori ground her teeth and prayed for patience. She had fought this particular fight with Betsy many times before. "Akro is one of our biggest clients, and for some unknown reason, no one can handle Karl like me. He's a son of a bitch, but he knows I'll get the job done. He's my ticket into the partnership, Betsy. All I have to do is keep him happy."

Betsy heaved herself out of the chair and walked back to her cubicle on the other side of the hall, shaking her head as she went. "Whatever you say, boss. Whatever you say."

• • •

The sun was throwing a curtain of pink across the horizon and the air was turning cool when Tori finally slid into the seat of her black and white Mini. A mountain of manila folders and heavy black binders—bedtime reading to prepare for her meeting with Karl—overflowed the passenger seat, along with the crystal vase and its cargo of roses. Their sensual fragrance overwhelmed the small space. Ella Fitzgerald's voice slid through the car as Tori turned the key, and she sat still for a moment, instantly transported back to Brit's Mercedes.

I should call him.
I definitely should not call him.
I should have slept with him.
You were out of your league. Let it go.

She pulled out of the parking garage, her thoughts running in circles as she followed the familiar path to the Langston Estates nursing home. When she arrived, the last rosy sunbeams were glancing off the side of the small brick building and lighting the shiny wintergreen shrubs growing beside it. She pulled into the small parking lot and threw open the car door. The damp air had awakened the smell of the lavender growing along the front walk. It helped clear the jumble in her head.

Tori pushed a button on the wall and braced herself for battle.

"Sorry, we're closed to visitors right now," came a stern

voice through a silver intercom.

"Chad, it's Tori Anderson. Any chance you could let me in to see my mom?" Tori stared into the shiny, black square above the intercom that she knew concealed a camera, and tried to look pitiful.

"Visiting hours are from nine to five, Tori. You know that." The regular night clerk sounded disgruntled, but that had never stopped him from letting her in before.

"Come on, Chad," Tori cajoled. "You know I can never get here during visiting hours. Besides, it's time for *I Love Lucy*. I know she's watching. Can't I stop in for a second? I promise I won't be in your hair."

There was a long pause.

"Pretty please? I'll bring you a triple mocha with extra whipped cream next time I come."

Still no response. Tori bit her lip and shifted from one foot to the other. Damn it, she knew she should have stopped on the way for the mocha. That always worked.

"Okay, but you owe me huge."

A buzzer announced that the door was unlocked. She swung it open with a sigh of relief. The hall inside was muted orange, the colors in the comfortable waiting room an autumn palate of rust, brown, yellow, and red. Langston Estates, a nursing care facility specializing in dementia and late-stage Alzheimer's disease, refused to treat its residents like patients in a hospital. It surrounded them with bright colors, music, and activities from poetry readings to plays.

"She's in the rec room." Chad greeted Tori halfway down the hall. The thin, stooped man had a kind spirit that he tried to disguise behind his brusque voice. "You better be in and out before nine. I'm not getting in trouble because you can't get here when you're supposed to."

Tori patted his arm gratefully. "You are a saint."

He snorted. "You been working late again?"

"Always," she said, trying to inject a cheerful note into her voice. "I got back this afternoon from Texas, via Florida and New York."

"Hmph. Doesn't seem right, a young thing like you spending all her time working."

"How's she been?"

"It's been a tough week," he said after a pause. "She hasn't wanted to eat much. But they've been working with her. I think she got out for a walk this morning, and that always helps her appetite."

With only thirty residents, the staff at Langston got to know all of the patients. Chad had a special rapport with the ladies. Tori had seen him coax a smile from her mother when no one else could communicate with her.

"Thanks, Chad."

Chad thrust a bony finger her direction. "You sure I can't fix you up with my cousin's boy Drake? He's a few years younger than you, but a nice boy. You'd like him."

"Sorry, gotta run. I've only got a few minutes, you know!" Tori patted his elbow and started toward the large common area that held two televisions and a library of books and magazines. Over the last year, Chad had offered to set her up with his cousin's sons, a neighbor, and two doctors who visited the home on occasion. Tori refused them all. Blind dates were not her cup of tea.

She hightailed it down the hall, a smile lingering around her lips. The familiar theme from *I Love Lucy* blared out at her the minute she passed through the wide double doors. Four or five residents sat on couches and in chairs watching the flickering lights of the television, their faces reflecting varying degrees of interest and comprehension. A watchful staff member sat at a large table on the other side of the television, playing cards with a gray-haired man with a thick white beard. He raised a hand to acknowledge Tori, and she waved back before approaching her mother.

"Hi, Mr. Barnes. Hi, Mom, it's me, Tori." She waited for them to acknowledge her before she lowered herself onto the couch to the right of a white-haired gentleman. Her mother sat to his left. Though Tori always expected it to get easier, nervous tension cramped her stomach as her mother turned vague, uncertain eyes in her direction. It was always a shock to see how frail she had become, her formerly plump, matronly figure whittled down to less than a hundred pounds, her hair white and thin.

Jeanne Anderson had once been a secretary, and the slow creep of Alzheimer's had become noticeable when she started to forget appointments and messages left for her boss. She had been diagnosed about the same time Tori was offered the Supreme Court clerkship. With no other family around, and her mother devastated by the diagnosis, Tori couldn't bear to tell her about the offer. The clerkship would have required relocating to D.C., something that would have been difficult for her increasingly nervous and forgetful mother. So Tori took a job with Hartner Lennigan, a firm her favorite professor recommended, and said good-bye to the Court.

Her first four years after law school had been a blur as Tori juggled doctor's appointments, part-time nurses, and her mother's growing need for supervision. She couldn't afford to give up her job, especially not with the prospect of full-time nursing care in her mother's future, but neither could she afford to leave her mother alone. So she worked at home when she could, drank untold cups of coffee, and managed to put in the hours her supervisors demanded.

Jeanne's descent through the stages of the disease had been relatively slow, and her fierce, stubborn pride always resisted Tori taking care of her. She argued vociferously for Tori to find nurses and other caretakers to stay with her, so her disease did not interfere with Tori's career. Then, six months ago, she asked to be placed in a nursing home.

The pain that simple request had caused Tori was immeasurable. All her life, Tori had been trying to please her mother, to make up for the pain she had suffered when Tori's dad had left them. But nothing Tori did seemed good enough. When she found out about Jeanne's illness, for one horrible moment Tori actually hoped it might bring them closer together. It did exactly the opposite. Never a demonstrative woman, Jeanne's struggle with Alzheimer's caused her to retreat into herself. She became cold and unresponsive, sharing few of her emotions with Tori. Though Tori wanted desperately to make her mother happy, she came to feel as though she was taking care of a stranger.

Their occasional hugs became fewer and far between, until Tori stopped expecting to be touched at all. In the past month, Jeanne had gone from forgetting Tori's name to seeing her as a familiar but unplaceable stranger.

"Hi, Tori." Mr. Barnes replied first. He was younger than her mother, in his mid-sixties, and had come to live at Langston Estates when his wandering had taken him miles from home one night, only his medical alert bracelet enabling a police officer to return him to his family.

Jeanne gave her a polite nod, though a light of recognition never flared in her eyes. She turned back to the television as the program came back on.

The three of them sat on the couch in silence.

"What have you been up to, Tori?" Mr. Barnes asked.

"Working." Tori tore her eyes from her mother's profile and gave him a sad smile. "I was in New York this morning negotiating a big contract."

Jeanne brightened. "I always say a woman has to have a career. Men will come and go and break your heart, but a woman's career is forever."

"You bet, Mom," Tori said. She'd heard that quote from

her mother more times than she could count. It was the one thing Alzheimer's couldn't seem to erase from her mind. "I wouldn't dream of it. They moved me into a corner office a few weeks ago. There's a real nice view. I wish you could see it."

"What is it you do again?" Mr. Barnes asked.

"I'm a lawyer," Tori replied. "I hope to make partner in a couple of years."

"Oh, now that would be excellent." Jeanne smiled. "Partner in a law firm. That's a real career. That's something to be proud of." She glanced at Tori for a moment before her attention drifted back to the television.

I'm doing it for you, Mom. Will you even remember me when it happens?

After all these years of working and struggling, would her mother even know when she made it to the top?

· · ·

When the last of the credits flickered across the screen, Tori stood up and stretched. "I'll see you in a couple of days, okay?" She stood beside her mother and touched her gently on the shoulder, but Jeanne shied away, looking uncomfortable. Tori bit her lip and tried not to react visibly. "Okay, then, in a couple of days."

She threw her purse over her shoulder and hurried out of the room. Chad leaned over and handed her a tissue as she walked past the desk.

"You'll be home for a while?" he asked.

She waved him off, not taking the tissue. She couldn't remember the last time she'd cried. Sometimes she wondered if the tears had all dried up. "I'll be around."

"Take care of yourself." He pushed a switch behind the counter and the front door buzzed open. "And think about Drake. He's a real nice boy."

Chapter Seven

Tori nervously adjusted the jacket of her tailored black suit, glancing up every few seconds to check the door.

Checking for him, of course.

Sunlight bounced off the New York skyline and splashed across the table of the Excorp boardroom, while an annoying cadre of lawyers grinned at her from the other side. Everyone loved a closing. They would do a final read-through of the documents, put pen to paper half a dozen times, and the deal would be done.

The only thing missing now was The Slayer.

Jerry Tollefson drummed his fingers on the table next to her. For all his talk of becoming a millionaire and flying to Maui, he had been strangely subdued during the trip to New York. Technix was the first company he'd started, and selling had to be difficult.

She stared glumly at a broken fingernail and fought the urge to bite it. Not exactly professional, biting one's fingernails during a business meeting. She put her hands in her lap instead, then leaned over to her briefcase and pulled out her BlackBerry to check her messages.

Two weeks had passed since she'd seen him, and her level of anxiety over this moment had been rising ever since. She'd considered launching into a total makeover, complete with diet, workout regimen, and new highlights, but had abandoned the idea after one excruciating kettlebell class at her local gym.

Some women had killer abs; Tori had a killer vocabulary.

Life was about trade-offs.

"Tori." Jerry leaned over to whisper in her ear. "You checked your messages ten seconds ago. If you don't stop fidgeting, I'm going to lose my mind."

"I'm not fidgeting. I'm working."

He sighed. "Whatever you're doing, cut it out. You're making me nervous."

The opening of the door saved Tori from responding. Brit walked in a second later, and she took in his raw masculinity like a blow to the stomach. A silent, strangled breath later, she forced a smile to her face and crossed the room to greet him.

Had she thought he looked good in his casual khakis and sweater? That was nothing. Today he had on a dark suit that emphasized the width of his shoulders and the narrowness of his waist. His thick hair, the hair that Tori remembered burying her fingers in, curled obediently back from his forehead while he surveyed her from head to toe, lingering on her narrow, pointed heels before traveling up her legs. She could have sworn a blue flame lit his eyes for a moment when they met her gaze, but then it was replaced with a polite look of disinterest.

What did that momentary light in his eyes mean? Could it be desire? Her knees suddenly felt weak.

Snap out of it, you idiot! Focus!

Her objective today was to sign the papers and get the

hell out of New York before she had time to think about how desperately she wanted to sleep with Brit. No second-guessing lights in his eyes. No thinking about strong hands, or slow, hot kisses.

You aren't his type and he isn't yours. Reject him before he rejects you.

"Mr. Bencher, how nice to see you. I'd like to introduce my client, Jerry Tollefson." Tori tried to keep her voice friendly and professional, yet somehow it came out sounding like a nervous teenage girl.

"Tori." Brit approached her first, shaking one hand and placing the other on top in a friendly gesture no one could question. Yet it affected her as much as if he had dragged her body against his. She tried to pull away but he did not release her for what seemed like an eternity. Their eyes met, and Tori nearly stumbled at the intensity of his gaze.

At least today she had worn the padded bra.

Brit turned to Jerry, stretching out his hand after finally releasing hers. "Jerry, I've been looking forward to meeting you. You've developed a hell of a company and I'm excited about bringing Technix and all it offers into the Excorp family."

Funny how he could use the word "family" and make it sound dangerously sexy, Tori thought, a bubble of hysteria building in her chest.

Jerry appraised Brit with a slow, thorough stare. "And I'm excited about becoming a millionaire." He grinned, but the smile looked forced. "Just don't do anything stupid with Technix, all right?"

"Stupid?" Brit asked, one dark eyebrow curling up.

"You know, don't break it up, lay off all my employees, or send it into bankruptcy. That sort of thing." For once, Jerry's eyes weren't crinkling with laughter.

Tori recognized the very real tension that underlay

Jerry's speech. After eight years of nonstop work, Jerry had burned himself out running Technix and needed to sell it to reclaim his life. But that didn't mean he had given up on his employees, or on the legacy he had built.

"Excorp doesn't play those games. When I buy a company, it's because the company's strong enough to stand on its own. I have no intention of doing anything other than offering Excorp's resources and letting Technix continue to operate as an independent entity."

"Jerry wouldn't have considered your offer if Excorp's reputation wasn't exactly that," Tori put in, hoping to remind Jerry of all the work they had done assessing Excorp and Brit Bencher. Brit had a reputation for guiding his companies when they needed help and leaving them on their own when they didn't. To Tori's knowledge, he had never bought and "flipped" a business for short-term profit. "We're trusting you to be a good shepherd to Technix."

Brit acknowledged the compliment with the barest inclination of his head. "Why don't we get started?" he said, extending his hand back toward the table. "I'm already looking forward to the handshake that closes this deal."

Jerry nodded and headed back to his seat.

Tori held her breath as Brit turned her direction. She started to follow Jerry, but froze when she heard Brit whisper her name in the painfully smooth voice that sent a shiver down her spine.

"Tori," he murmured, softly enough that she doubted anyone else could hear. "Miss me?"

Her stomach dropped and she spun around. "Let's keep this professional, shall we?" She looked around to see if they were getting any odd looks from the other men assembled around the table. A secretary entered with a stack of documents that she took to Harold. Everyone's attention turned to him as he began identifying each of the key documents necessary to close the transaction.

"Who said anything about being unprofessional? You, *Ms. Anderson*, are the epitome of professional. Even your e-mails are professional." He cleared his throat. "'Dear Brit, thank you for the flowers. I would appreciate your efforts to close the Technix deal forthwith. Cordially, Tori.'" He gave a low chuckle.

"I did not say 'forthwith'," she whispered, her eyebrows raising with indignation. "No decent attorney under the age of sixty uses the word 'forthwith.'"

"That's too bad." He tapped his chin. "What if I said I would like to take you back to your hotel forthwith and finish what we started?"

She gasped and heat flooded her cheeks. Of all the ways she had imagined Brit greeting her, blatant sexual innuendo had never even entered her mind. It was as astonishing as it was infuriating. She was a professional, first and foremost. She couldn't stand around flirting with Brit in the middle of a meeting.

"We are here for a very important business transaction, Mr. Bencher. I assumed you would be mature enough to recognize that."

"Mature? I don't believe I've ever been called that before."

"Perhaps because you aren't?"

"You're tough," Brit said. "I like that."

The gleam in his eye sent a pulse throbbing at the base of her throat. She brushed a strand of hair back from her face and cleared her throat. "Is there any chance we can forget that night ever happened?"

"If only I could," he said, eyes dripping with sorrow. "But you said, and I quote, 'Maybe another time.' Those words haunt me, Tori. They haunt me."

She stifled a smile. "Figure of speech. Polite conversation."

He made a tsk-ing sound. "Are you saying you lied to me?"

"I said maybe. I didn't promise anything."

"You implied it." He took a step closer, and she could smell his cologne. The scent was dark, spicy, and sexy. Like Brit.

Damn it!

Tori's mouth watered. "Implication doesn't create an obligation."

"I can't tell you how much it turns me on when you speak lawyer."

"You're insane."

"Only because you made me this way."

Tori quivered with laughter. "Does Harold turn you on, too?"

Brit leaned in a few inches from her ear. "You can't imagine."

Tori noticed they were starting to get a few curious looks, including one from Jerry. She backed away. "What will it take to make you leave me alone?"

"You," he said simply. "I want you."

• • •

For the next few hours, Tori focused on getting through the meeting as quickly and painlessly as possible. Despite the flowers and the note, she had assumed Brit wouldn't want a repeat of last week. Betsy would chalk it up to hopeless insecurity, but the longer she thought about it, the more impossible anything between them became.

Yet there he was—flirting with her. Flirting! Tori alternated between shock, terror, and raging lust. She finally had to resort to clutching her coffee cup or leaving her hands in her lap to disguise the tremble in her hands whenever he addressed her. His masculine fragrance drifted across the room, lingering under her nose, and each scent took her back to her hotel room, when his kisses had set her body on fire.

When the meeting was finally over, Tori sighed with relief as she threw her documents into her briefcase and prepared to leave. She could barely focus on the deal long enough to celebrate the closing with a smile and a round of handshakes. She had no idea what Brit would say or do next, and had decided her only recourse was to flee as quickly as possible.

If Brit really wanted to see her again, he could call her. He did not need to seduce her between cups of coffee with Harold and stilted conversations about the weather.

She watched Brit excuse himself from the conference table and join Jerry by the pastries. Jerry ate more like a fifteen-year-old boy than a grown man. It would have been endearing, if it weren't so annoying to watch him feed his face and never gain a pound.

Brit and Jerry had struck up an immediate rapport, and it was apparent in the now-easy set to Jerry's shoulders. Both were smart, driven, and incredibly good at their chosen professions, though Jerry tended toward the beach-bum end of the spectrum and Brit toward the perfectly groomed CEO. Given the right circumstances, they probably would have become friends.

Jerry motioned for Tori to join them as he took a large bite from a cherry Danish. She sighed, pasted an artificial smile on her face, and threw her briefcase over her shoulder.

Stay calm, Tori. You can do this.

"So Brit, Tori and I have a few hours in the city before our train leaves. Any suggestions? A few tourist attractions we should hit before we leave?" Jerry flashed his trademark smile, his body a relaxed slouch now that the deal was finally complete.

"You haven't been to New York before?"

"I know it's hard to believe, but when I have an opportunity to take a vacation, I tend to do it somewhere the car-to-human ratio is a bit lower." Jerry popped the remainder of the Danish into his mouth and continued. "Tori used to live here, but she never takes vacations. I imagine you could pick almost anything and we'd never have seen it."

Tori contemplated kicking her client. She'd told him she'd had a perfectly nice dinner with Brit but that was all, and he'd been too much of a gentleman to inquire further. But she had the feeling he wasn't going to let her leave town without comment.

"I've seen the Statue of Liberty," she said. It had been a work function with a bunch of other summer associates, but she had gone.

"It doesn't count if you were looking at your BlackBerry the whole time," Brit said. "You actually have to turn that thing off to appreciate the sight."

Tori's mouth dropped open, but she couldn't think of a retort.

Jerry let out a hoot of laughter. "He's got your number!"

"Do your e-mails read themselves?" she asked.

"No, but apparently they're much more patient than yours," Brit said. "Sometimes they let me go hours without reading them."

A buzz from Tori's waist interrupted the conversation. Brit and Jerry laughed while her face burned. With some effort, she ignored what was probably an irritated message from Karl Bulcher, demanding to know when she'd be back in town.

"You'd need a week or more to really get to know the city. When do you leave?" Brit asked.

"We weren't sure how late things would run, so we're not out until seven tonight," Jerry replied.

Tori stared at the leather stitching around the edge of

her shoes to avoid meeting Brit's eyes. "Six forty-five," she corrected. "But we want to get there nice and early. It's a full train and I want a seat in the quiet car. I have a lot to do."

Don't embarrass me, Jerry. Please.

Brit glanced at the heavy silver Rolex at his wrist. "It's only noon. Plenty of time. Why don't I take you for a quick tour of the city?"

"That sounds lov—" Jerry began.

"We may be able to get out earlier if we go to the station now," Tori said. The last thing in the world she needed was to sit in a small car with Brit. "Much as I appreciate the offer, I don't think it's a good idea."

"But we've got reservations on the Acela," Jerry said, grinning all the wider. "I refuse to ride any other train. Besides, it's not every day you get the opportunity to see the city with such a distinguished guide. Tori, you blocked out the day on your calendar, didn't you?"

What was he thinking? Tori narrowed her gaze. As Jerry slid his hands in his pockets, he could not have looked more like the cat that swallowed the canary.

He was trying to set her up.

"Maybe. That doesn't mean I don't have work to do," she said.

"I promise I'll get you to the station on time," Brit told her, one hand reaching out briefly to touch her elbow.

The contact shot through her like a painful, tingling shock. She gritted her teeth and maintained the smile. "How very kind of you."

"No problem at all," Brit replied. He motioned toward a phone on a table against the wall. "Please excuse me for a moment. I'll have something set up for us."

When he stepped away, Tori glared at Jerry. "What are you thinking? Are you trying to throw me at him?"

Jerry feigned astonishment. "What do you mean? You

told me you two had a perfectly nice dinner. You're friends now, right?"

Tori glanced away. "Friends isn't really the right word."

"Surely not more than friends?" Jerry widened his eyes.

"Well…" Tori adjusted her bag on her shoulder.

Jerry chuckled. "Betsy told me about the roses. A very nice touch."

"Betsy told you *what*?" She had taken the roses home specifically to avoid comments and questions. Betsy was in huge trouble.

"I am a little hurt that you didn't tell me personally, but really, I don't mind gossiping with your secretary."

Great, now she was being punished for telling Betsy about Brit, but not Jerry. She should have known the two would talk about her.

Brit hung up the phone and rejoined them, forestalling her response. "My assistant is working out the details. First, we need lunch. After that, a quick trip to the Museum of Modern Art. I never miss an opportunity to look at *The Starry Night*. That should give us time to get to the helipad at four, and we'll get you to your train after that."

"Helipad?" Jerry asked, his blond eyebrows twitching with interest.

"The only way to see the city if you're on a short timeline. We'll fly by the Empire State building and check out Ms. Liberty close up. You'll love it."

"Those things don't look safe," Tori said. "Are there even seatbelts in a helicopter? I made a resolution this year never to wear a parachute to work."

"You won't be jumping out," Brit said. "You'll be sitting in a comfortable seat. Looking at the sites. It's actually very peaceful."

"I prefer to see my sites from the ground," Tori said.

"What are you talking about?" Jerry asked. "The

other day you were telling me how you loved going up to the observation deck on top of City Hall. You said it felt peaceful."

"That's different. That's not a helicopter," she said.

"You'll be fine." Brit motioned toward the door. "We'd better get going. We've got a lot to do."

Tori turned her back on both men. She was being outmaneuvered, and she didn't like it one bit.

Chapter Eight

As much as Tori was determined to stay irritated with Jerry, lunch proved lighthearted and enjoyable. They dined at a restaurant called Verve, a tiny establishment with an air of exclusivity and a cheerful, colorful décor. The tables were art deco red, the chairs a lemony yellow, and expressive, abstract paintings covered the walls. They were the only people in the room wearing suits. Tori saw a woman carrying a baby in a backpack, and a gorgeous couple she could have sworn had appeared in a previous week's edition of *People* magazine.

The prices would have made Tori gasp if Brit had not insisted on footing the bill. She ordered a panini sandwich with a pesto aioli that made her mouth tingle with the perfect combination of basil and garlic, and a salad of grated root vegetables. Jerry feasted on a pork sandwich served with a pineapple and cranberry chutney and thick, homemade french fries.

As she expected, Brit and Jerry had a lot in common. They traded insults about each other's sports teams and discussed their running regimens (both had completed a marathon years ago, but agreed that their "old" bones didn't relish the activity the way they once had). Tori stayed quiet and observed Brit. Though he had shed his air of businesslike reserve within minutes of leaving the Excorp building, he retained the mantle of power and authority, easily commanding the attention of everyone around him. The owner of the restaurant, Sam Huo, came out to say hello after their meal had been served. He was a thin, animated man with a heavy accent and a habit of kissing the hand of every woman who entered the restaurant.

Jerry seemed to delight in poking fun at Brit, which was the best evidence that he was enjoying Brit's company. He asked Brit about the rumor that Excorp was planning to buy Starbucks to cement its plans for world domination, and questioned the need for a private health club, complete with squash courts and a swimming pool, in the basement of the Excorp tower.

Brit handled it all with a good-natured smile. After enduring a number of pointed comments from Jerry, he turned things around and began to ask questions of his own. "Tell me more about Technix," he said, in that soft voice that was only inches from being a command. "I know what's in your materials, but tell me the real story. How you got started. Surely there's an interesting twist or two in there."

He spoke primarily to Jerry. Tori had been avoiding the conversation by eating far more than she wanted or intended. Any time Brit asked her a question, she shook her head and pointed to her full mouth to excuse her inability to speak.

The truth was, she had no idea how to handle the situation. Brit was devilishly smart, confident, and attractive. She couldn't bring herself to believe he truly wanted her. And even if she could, what then? Did she really have the guts to have a fling with a man like Brit?

Tori shoved the tail end of her sandwich into her mouth.

"It's really not particularly exciting," Jerry said. "Technix began as an idea in my basement. I wanted to combine my work at Columbia in artificial intelligence with the computer security field. I had no idea what I was doing. In that, Technix wasn't very different than any other high-tech start-up. The difference for me was having a great lawyer." Jerry patted Tori's shoulder. "Tori understood my dream. She got me financing when everyone said my idea for a new type of security software was a pipe dream. Had to go to Japan and Australia to do it, but Tori's a bulldog. We went through two rounds of investing before the technology was commercial, and two more after that. You've purchased the product of four years of sleepless nights, for both me and Tori."

Tori swallowed the last bite of her salad hastily, feeling compelled to speak. "Don't let Jerry fool you. He showed me his designs for an AI security system, and I knew I wanted to be involved. Technix was too good to stay hidden for long. I was lucky he let me represent the company."

"Quit trying to be modest," Jerry said. "I don't know how many hours you put in for free. It's not like you were being paid for travel time."

"It's not like I was being paid for anything," Tori said drily. In the beginning, Jerry didn't have more than the shirt on his back, a fantastic idea, and the skill and intelligence to make that dream come true. She didn't charge him for years. "Money had nothing to do with it. I knew Jerry deserved to succeed, and I wanted to be there when he did."

"And so you are," Brit said. "Sounds like you've been a busy woman for the past few years, Tori. It isn't as though Technix was your only client."

"I can't imagine anything I'd rather be doing than working with people like Jerry," she said truthfully.

Brit tapped one long finger on the top of his glass. "Really?" he drawled. "I can think of lots of things I'd rather do than work."

Tori bent over her plate. Damn it, nothing left to eat. She took a long drink of water instead.

"Not Tori," Jerry said. "She's a machine. I've never seen her miss a day of work, except when her mother—"

"Goodness, it is getting late," Tori said, pointing at her watch with a fake smile. "We'll want to leave soon if we expect to get through MoMA." She kicked Jerry under the table. Her mother was private business. Brit Bencher certainly didn't need to know about her. But Jerry wasn't paying any attention. The theme from *Star Wars*—his favorite movie— filled the air. He pulled his cell phone out of a pocket and answered as he moved away from the table.

"You and Jerry seem to have formed a mutual admiration society." Brit folded his napkin and placed it on his empty plate, then leaned back in his chair.

"Yes, we're very close." Tori had a sudden, delicious fantasy of seeing Brit jealous over her relationship with Jerry.

"How close?" he asked.

"Very close," she repeated, though with less conviction. She wished she had the courage to spin a good story, but unfortunately, Jerry would not be above exposing her lie, if Brit brought it up.

"I see." Brit smiled with satisfaction. "So you aren't..."

"I don't believe that's any of your business."

His smile grew wider. "Of course it is. I like Jerry. I wouldn't want to poach in his territory."

"Oh, that's vile." She dropped her napkin on the table. "As if I'm some sort of possession the two of you could split between you."

"Not at all," he protested. "I never had any intention of splitting you. Perhaps I haven't made myself clear. I want you all to myself." He reached across the table to brush his fingers against hers.

She shied and pulled away, crossing her legs and pushing back from the table. "Look," she said, "I'm here with Jerry. This really isn't a good time."

"Not a good time?" The suggestive gleam in his eyes made Tori dig her nails into her palm. "What about later tonight?"

"Perhaps you didn't hear me earlier. I've got a reservation. On a train. Back to Philadelphia."

Brit tapped his finger against his mouth as he observed her. "There's a jazz trio playing at the Club Hantro this evening that I know you'll like. Forget the train. Stay with me."

Tori's stomach dropped into her toes. This was it. No more stalling.

Stay, or go?

Jerry reappeared, saving her once again from the decision. His mouth was pinched, a high flush staining his cheekbones. "That was Cindy. She's in trouble again."

Tori melted. "Oh no, I'm so sorry." Jerry's troubled younger sister Cindy bounced between drug rehab and jail, with a good dose of trouble thrown in at either end.

"She's in Houston. I'm going straight to the airport and getting the first flight there."

Brit didn't ask questions. He rose and pulled out his phone. "I'll talk to my assistant. I think we've got an Excorp jet headed there this afternoon. Let me take care of it."

Twenty minutes later, Jerry was in a cab on his way to Kennedy while Brit and Tori sat back down to finish their coffee at Verve. Tori watched Jerry go with mixed emotions—scared for him, terrified for herself. She was now alone with Brit—and the last of her excuses for putting him off had vanished.

"So," he asked, as soon as they were alone. "You're staying, right?"

His raw confidence dragged across Tori's pride like a set of nails down a chalkboard. "Actually," she drawled, stirring one more lump of sugar into her coffee, "I'm not sure I can. I had planned to go into the office this weekend."

"But you won't."

"I won't?" she repeated, feeling the heat rise in her cheeks. "Says who?"

"Tori." He sounded patient, weary. "This is getting silly. We are going to look at some art and take a tour of the city. Then we're going to go back to my apartment and finish what we started last week."

"Hmph." She crossed her arms over her chest. "Women do whatever you want, don't they?"

"Not all the time. Sometimes they say 'maybe another time' and leave me wanting."

So polished. So perfect. And I'm supposed to believe this crap?

"Are you determined to scowl at me like that?" Brit asked.

She pushed out her chin. "Yes. And if you don't like it, you can send me back to Philly right now."

"Well then, I'm afraid you've forced me to do this." He stood up and held out his hand.

She stared at it suspiciously. "What?"

"Come with me." He wiggled his fingers.

"Where?"

"To Sam's office. He won't mind. We've got to get something straight between us."

Tori swallowed, hard. Brit's jaw hardened as he waited for her to take his hand. Something compelled her to drop her palm into his. She closed her eyes at the warm sensation that followed.

Stumbling, she allowed him to lead her back through the kitchen. It was an open room almost as big as the restaurant, filled with the odors of garlic, hot oil, and baking bread. Enormous skylights bathed them in bright sunlight. Sam was there, talking to a man who was cleaning a stainless steel countertop that stretched the length of the room.

"Sam, do you mind if we borrow your office?" Brit asked.

"Of course not," Sam replied, the hint of a question in his barely raised eyebrows.

"We won't be long."

Tori gritted her teeth and resisted the urge to take back her hand and run out of the restaurant. But, damn her cowardly soul, she didn't have the guts to make a scene, and she had the feeling Brit wouldn't let her get away so easily. He led her to a private office with an oversized leather armchair in one corner and a tidy desk in another. A light with a beaded shade cast a soft glow in the small space, and a faint odor of incense gave the room an exotic feel. Brit closed the door behind them and turned the lock.

Tori backed against the desk, immediately pinned by the intensity of Brit's stare. "So, what—" Her voice trembled and she cleared her throat before beginning again. "What exactly did you want to tell me?"

"I don't want to tell you anything. I said we had something we needed to get straight. This is it."

Chapter Nine

Brit did not hesitate before wrapping his arms around Tori and drawing her delicious body into a tight embrace. He'd been wanting to do it since he saw her that morning, and at the moment, he wasn't particularly interested in butterfly kisses and gentle foreplay. He wanted to drink in her perfume, her scent of roses and jasmine, until he was dizzy with need. He wanted to bury himself between her thighs until she moaned, her voice a husky, strangled whisper, as it had been that night in the car.

He kissed Tori with all the repressed energy that had come from two weeks of wanting…and frustration. He wasn't supposed to be the one feeling this way. He slept with models, actresses, women who could make a man's head spin with one flick of a finger. But it was Tori he could not stop thinking about. Tori, with her halo of honey-blond hair, dark coffee eyes that snapped with intelligence and wit, and small, curvy body that fit inside the crook of his arm.

He'd been stunned when she turned him down, and shocked that he'd let his own interest in Tori distract him from his reason for taking her out in the first place. Of course he hadn't pressed her about staying the night—even for Melissa, he wasn't going to seduce an unwilling woman. But his worries about his sister had only compounded over the past two weeks. He was failing. Failing to protect Melissa and failing in his role as family caretaker.

Meanwhile, success lay in the arms of Tori Anderson.

But now that he had her all to himself, he had to admit that last thing he wanted to think about was his sister.

He noticed with satisfaction that Tori did not hesitate before responding to his kiss. For all her words of protest, she couldn't subdue her body. The other night he had felt hesitation trembling in her veins, nervousness over what they were about to do. There was none of that now.

Her hands clutched at his shoulders and she gripped him as tightly as he held her. He nudged her back, against the table, until she rested on the edge, her knees parting to give him room. Ah, it was sweet heaven there, between her legs, the juncture of her thighs creating a perfect home for his hard sex. Her hips arched, bringing them closer together, and he smiled against her neck.

He pulled back enough to remove her jacket and let his fingers slide across her breasts. Firm nipples moved under his searching hands and she moaned. The sound made his groin tighten. He played gently with the delicate points and as he did she spread her legs wider, her head falling back against her shoulders.

She was heat and fire, everything he had experienced two weeks ago. But this time, he wasn't letting her slip away.

He dropped his fingers lower, letting his mouth caress her neck and the curve of her collarbone as his hand drifted under her skirt to the warmth of her mound. The fabric bunched around her hips as he pushed it higher, and again higher, until he finally had unencumbered access to crinkling hair that tickled his fingers through the smooth silk of her underwear. She bucked against his hand, and he took that for an invitation to go deeper. His slid his fingers under the top of the elastic, tangled for a moment in her wiry curls, and then moved lower. With one finger he parted the soft skin and could not prevent a groan when he felt the slick nub below. She was hot, wet, and ready for him.

Damn it. He suppressed another groan, this one of frustration. He hadn't put a condom in his wallet that morning.

Grimly, he swallowed his own aching desire and focused on Tori. He let his fingers slide in a circle around her clit, noting the spots that made her jump, arch, and push harder against him. He teased her until her hips began to move rhythmically against him.

"Brit, we shouldn't…" a garbled whisper came from Tori.

"Lean back," he urged. "Let me take care of you." A moment later, she put her hands behind her on the desk and opened her legs farther, her skirt now around her waist, her position one of perfect abandon. He got down on his knees and gently pulled down the tiny silk thong, leaving a path of kisses on her inner thighs and calves. He slipped off her shoes and gently massaged the arch of each foot. She had soft pink toenails. They were perfectly Tori—professional, yet feminine. He kissed each toe.

"What about—"

"Tori." He kissed her ankle. "Shut." He kissed the back of her knee. "Up."

He brought one hand back up her inner thigh. He allowed one finger to slide over the wet nub and then gently penetrate her.

She gasped with pleasure. He moved his finger in and then out, imagining as he did that it was his cock and not his finger that was swallowed by her heat. Her hips began to move faster and he pulled out.

"Not yet," he murmured. If he wasn't going to have his own release, then by God he was going to enjoy hers. He put one hand on either side of her nether lips, spreading her before him like a red canna from a Georgia O'Keeffe painting. Then, with a deep sigh of pleasure, he leaned forward.

Her deep, musky fragrance reached him first, shooting straight from his nose to his groin. Then her taste rolled over his tongue. She was like an aged cabernet, rich and sweet, blackberries and espresso mixing with the raw hunger of sexual need.

Each exhalation came on a moan, her thighs tightening spasmodically around him. He drank deeply of her wine, inhaling her even as she thrust harder against him. He nibbled at her, tickling the nub of her desire as he did, then slid his tongue along her.

With one trembling hand, she pushed his head firmly against her. "Please," she urged. "Please, I can't take any more."

With two fingers, he traced the path his cock was so desperate to take, and at the same time, sucked hard. She came in a burst, a cry of pure pleasure filling the room as she jerked against him. He kept moving, sucking, until the shaking stopped, and her body went limp in his arms.

• • •

When the world stopped spinning, Tori lifted her head and opened her eyes. Brit was on his knees, watching her with a steady, glowing hunger. It took her a moment to recall that her legs were spread wide, and her panties lay in a discarded heap on the floor.

What was he doing to her? She snapped her legs together and pushed herself off the edge of the desk, peeking behind as a hot blush crawled across her cheeks. Had she left a stain on the desk?

"No, my transparent beauty, you don't have to worry. The desk is fine." Brit slowly rose to his feet, watching her with that deep, measuring gaze.

Tori pushed her skirt back to her knees, barely able to believe the desire still running through her body. She wanted him again. Now. In a bed or on the desk, it didn't matter. She wet her lips.

Lord, what had she done? What was he doing to her?

He picked up her thong and handed it to her. "Someday you'll have to explain to me why women wear these things. Other than to torment men, that is."

Tori snatched the offending garment from his hand, her face burning hotter than before. "I haven't done laundry for a while," she said.

He jumped to his feet and caught her in a rough embrace. The length of his erection pressed against her thigh and she had to suppress an urge to open her legs and give him room. "Tori, I don't understand why you're fighting this. We're good together."

"I don't have time for this, Brit. My life is…complicated."

And, if we're being honest, you scare the crap out of me. All right?

"Tori, I want a weekend with you. That's it. No pressure."

She dropped her head against his chest, unable to face the knowing look she'd see in his eyes. Why *was* she fighting so hard? She had Brit Bencher between her thighs, for goodness sakes. He offered pleasure with no strings attached. No hard feelings when they rolled out of bed the next day and went their separate ways.

What was she so afraid of, anyway? She wasn't a helpless lamb being led to the slaughter. She was an adult, with a raging sensuality that had been locked up for far too long.

She had a sudden, irrational urge to call Betsy and ask what she should do. But she knew what Betsy would say. *Are you kidding? Have some fun for once,* her bubbly secretary would cry, throwing her hands up in despair. *He's offering you the chance of a lifetime. Take it!*

Unbidden, she heard her voice as if it was coming from a distance. "I suppose I could stay the night. But just the night. I've got work waiting for me at home."

With one large hand, he guided her face to his. "It's Friday. You'll stay the weekend. You can go back Monday."

"I'll leave early Sunday morning," she said stubbornly, looking at his shoulder.

He chuckled. "You've always got to have the last word, don't you?"

She pursed her lips and looked him directly in the eyes for the first time, a weight lifting from her shoulders when she saw the pleasure reflected there. No knowing look, no smug grin. Honest pleasure.

He was right. Why not stay? Why not give in to this unexpected and overwhelming desire? She'd be back to work soon enough, and Brit Bencher would be nothing more than a pleasant memory.

An answering smile reluctantly formed at the corner of her mouth. "It's one of my many personality flaws. I'm also moody and argumentative. At least, that's what my friends tell me."

"With friends like that, it's no wonder you need a weekend away. Sunday it is. But while you're here, no more pretending you don't want this as much as I do." He guided her hand down his chest to the erection that still lay heavy against her leg.

Unbidden, her fingers closed gently around him. She stroked him with a light touch, feeling herself throb with renewed pleasure when he closed his eyes and leaned against her. Her other hand settled on his shoulder, and she could feel the cords of muscles in his neck tighten as she gave in to the desire to rub her hips against him.

"I think we'll need to make a slight change of plans," he said a moment later, his voice tight. "I forgot something at home. We'll have to drop by my penthouse. I hope you don't mind."

Tori barely heard him, as she brought her other hand up to his shoulders and gently pushed him against the leather chair. "I don't think that will be necessary." She shoved hard and he fell into the seat. She grabbed her purse and pulled a fresh condom from the secret pocket in the back.

A good attorney is always prepared. Tori's Rules of Negotiation Number Four.

She'd refilled her stash the night after she returned home. Not because of Brit, of course. Because a woman had to be prepared.

When he saw what she had retrieved, he closed his eyes and sighed with pleasure. "How did you guess?"

She unbuttoned his pants with fingers that had suddenly become nimble with need. Later, she wanted to linger over his body, feel him slowly enter and fill her. But now she wanted it fast and hard. She wanted to forget everything about herself. Her job. The partnership. Long days and lonely nights.

After a few, impatient minutes, she had straddled him, her knees finding purchase in the smooth leather. She covered his mouth with a deep, searching kiss and tasted her own juices still lingering on his tongue.

How long had it been since she'd done this?

You've never *done this.*

"I can't wait," he said against her mouth.

"Don't try."

He tangled his fingers in her hair and kissed her hard, their teeth bumping in a tempest of passion. It was quick and hard. He drove into her with a fierce, needy rhythm, and she matched his every move. Though she had not though it possible, she felt her own pleasure rising and building. When she leaned back and arched her hips, he touched a place inside her that no man had ever reached, and it sent her reeling into space. Faster and faster they moved, until he groaned against her neck, his body tensing. When she felt him explode inside her, she let herself go as well. His relief was sudden and violent, and she shattered along with him, their bodies moving in unison. He shook with his release, his arms locking around her as he buried a cry of pleasure against her mouth.

They lay together, panting, until Tori's legs began to cramp. Reluctantly, she peeled herself off and stood on shaky legs. The embarrassment she had felt earlier disappeared, replaced by a flood of pure satisfaction.

"Now that we've got that settled..." She pulled the remaining pins from her hair and let it settle around her shoulders. "We should probably give Sam back his office."

"I should probably buy him a new chair," Brit said, crinkling his nose.

Tori laughed. Who knew sex could be so damn fun? After worrying all day about what to do with her overwhelming attraction, she now felt light, carefree.

Staring at the hard contours of Brit's face, Tori made a resolution. She would give herself this weekend—at least, until Sunday—to enjoy this reckless, impossible passion. Her work, Karl Bulcher, and her mother would all be waiting when she went back home. For now she'd forget it all.

It was no strings, no looking back, and no regrets.

• • •

They went to the museum first, but neither Tori nor Brit had the attention span to gaze solemnly at works of art. So they headed for Central Park instead, and spent hours walking around aimlessly in the warm sunshine. It seemed only natural that Brit would reach out and take her hand as he pulled her out of the path of a particularly unstable inline skater, and not let her go as they threaded their way around the groups of people enjoying the early summer warmth. They talked about nothing of importance. Books, plays, music they liked. When they reached the edge of Turtle Pond—one of the few places Tori remembered from her time in the city—Brit gallantly threw down his jacket and motioned for her sit on it.

"Are you sure?" Tori asked. She directed her gaze at the Armani tag.

Brit bowed. "What gentleman would not lay down his coat for a lady?"

Tori pulled off her own jacket and laid it beside his. "Ann Taylor," she said as she dropped on top of it. "Not nearly as much of a loss."

Brit gave her a mock frown as he settled next to her. "You can't subject everything to a financial risk analysis, you know. Sometimes you have to let a gentleman make a grand gesture."

Tori laughed. "I'll let you make the grand gesture when it matters. Like when we're on the helicopter."

He shuddered. "Goodness, that's morbid. I certainly hope I'm not required to make any sort of gesture, grand or otherwise, while we're a thousand feet in the air."

"I like to plan ahead." She leaned back on her arms. A small group of children threw sticks and pebbles into the water as their anxious mothers hovered behind. To their right, a group of boys played football in a grassy stretch at the edge of the Great Lawn. Their game seemed to center around tackling, as no one had much luck throwing or catching.

"I gathered that. You're a bit young to be handling transactions like this on your own, aren't you?" he said.

"Technix is my client," she said simply. "I'm not sure how they could stop me. And, I must admit, they make me run everything past one of the senior partners. Drives me crazy."

"That sounds like the story of your life," he observed. "I believe you're what some might call an overachiever."

Tori looked up, half-expecting to see disapproval, but only amusement radiated from his clear blue gaze. She pulled a clover from the grass and twirled it. "So I've heard."

"But no husband, no kids. Aren't you falling behind there?"

"What are you, the U.S. Census?"

"You're a beautiful, sexy woman. I'm simply noting that it's surprising some man hasn't tied you to his bed long before now."

"Hmm." She thought for a moment about being tied to Brit's bed. It was a nice thought. She shook her head to clear her mind. "Nope. I was engaged once, right out of law school, but he didn't seem to have any trouble giving me the boot. It was for the best. I really don't have time for a relationship. I'm going to apply for partner in a couple of years, and they'll be looking hard at my numbers. I can't afford to get lazy."

"Somehow, I doubt that will be a problem." He trailed one hand along the side of her calf. "I assume that means you aren't dating anyone?"

"Ha!" She found another clover and pulled off its lobes, one after another, studiously ignoring the delicious tickle of his fingers. "I don't even remember what that means. It's a relief, really. No one expects anything from me, or gets frustrated when I forget to come home for dinner." She gestured toward his hand. "But you must agree. I don't see a ring on your finger."

"I've got more family than I know what to do with," Brit said. "Two brothers, a sister, and countless nieces and nephews. The last thing I need is more family."

Tori laughed at his disgusted expression. "I forgot you had a sister. Tell me about her."

"She's a lot like you. Brilliant, driven...suspicious. She used to do research in a robotics lab out in Southern California. But then she went through a messy breakup, and a few months ago she moved out here. She's been having a hard time since then."

"I'm sorry to hear that."

A muscle flexed in his jaw, and a dark, cold anger burned in his eyes. "So am I."

Tori tried to lighten the suddenly dark mood. "Wait—I remind you of your sister? Doesn't that sound a tad creepy?"

He flashed a white-toothed grin. "No. Unless there's something creepy about appreciating strong women."

Unsure how to stop the rush of pleasure that followed from the compliment, Tori decided a change of subject was in order. "I love Central Park. I used to jog here all the time when I worked in the city. Did you come here a lot, when you were growing up?"

"Sometimes. My mother didn't like us to ride the subway alone. We found plenty of trouble to get into closer to home."

"Trouble?" She arched a brow. "Brit Bencher, in trouble?"

"Well, let's say we were lucky all we saw was the back of the truant officer's car, and not the red and blue lights. You'd be surprised what three brothers can do, without even trying."

"I see." She studied his profile and the smooth olive cast of his skin. "You know, it occurs to me that you never told me why they call you Brit. I saw the real name on the papers today, you know. John Bencher the Third."

He winced. "Some day, I'm going to change that. Legally, I mean."

"What's wrong with John? Seems like a perfectly reasonable name to me."

"If you don't mind following in your father's footsteps, perhaps."

She rolled over on her elbow. He stared off at the young children by the water, who had turned from rock throwing to heaving old crusts of bread at the ducks and squealing with delight when they honked at each other and fought over the white chunks.

"Didn't you? I mean, didn't you inherit Excorp from your father?"

"Yes and no. The company my grandfather founded manufactured radios. It was marginally successful and utterly boring. I had no interest in getting involved. I was interested in technology and high-risk projects with the potential for big payouts. My brothers nicknamed me Brit because I was fascinated with the UK. I even went through a period where I mimicked a Scottish accent, à la Sean Connery. I think I saw one too many James Bond flicks. I was determined to live there after I graduated from business school."

Now that was an amusing thought. Brit, trying to pull off a 007 impression. "And?" she prompted. "Did you?"

"No. For all my talk of living in Scotland, I've never spent more than a few nights there at a time." He laughed, but she could feel an undercurrent of tension in his voice, and see it in the sudden tautness of his jaw.

"What happened?"

"Life." He shrugged. "By the time I graduated from college the business wasn't doing well. My younger brothers were still in school. Dad was never a great businessman. He needed help. I did what I had to do. I reinvented Excorp, made some risky investments in our manufacturing process, and made us profitable. A few years later, we absorbed a couple of competitors and became even more profitable. Three years ago Excorp went public. It wasn't exactly what I expected to do with my life, but at least I've been able to make sure my folks are supported, and no one has to worry about money any longer."

"But no traveling?" she asked.

"Oh, I travel. I've been all over the world. The irony is, I rarely make it out of hotel conference rooms and high-rise office buildings."

Tori swallowed hard, remembering how her heart had dropped when she learned of her mother's diagnosis. How she struggled not to feel resentful for her lost opportunity, and the guilt that had piled up for thinking about herself when it was her mother who was suffering.

"I'm sorry," she offered, unsure how to respond to the unexpected intimacy of the moment.

He grinned, breaking the solemnity with unexpected humor. "Don't worry. I'm not dead yet. I figure there's still time. Someday, I'm going to Scotland. It will be the trip that fulfills all those childhood fantasies." He turned her hand over and tapped on her palm. "Now, I've told you about my name, so you've got to spill the beans about that clerkship. Remember?"

Tori froze. She'd never been good at talking about her family. What could say about her mother, anyway? Two nights ago, Jeanne had flown into a rage when Tori visited, screaming and throwing things until Tori left her room. The doctor said it was a common occurrence during the later stages of the disease. Ever since, Tori hadn't been able to think about her mother without a feeling of panic.

"I...um..." she tried to speak but it was no use. The pain hit like it always did—with the force of an earthquake that left her reeling. She struggled to regain her composure, rubbing hard across her eyes and clearing her throat.

Brit reached out and stroked her hand. "Hey, I didn't mean to put you on the spot. You don't have to answer."

Tori shook her head, her throat locking. His gentle touch

only made it worse. Damn it, she couldn't fall apart like this every time someone mentioned her mother.

She sucked in a deep breath and forced out the words. "My mother has Alzheimer's. She was diagnosed at the same time I found out about the clerkship. I never told her about it. We don't have any other family around, and it wouldn't have been a good time for her to move. So I went back home and got a job with Hartner. It was for the best. I like my job, and the money's good enough for me to pay for her care. That's all that really matters anyway."

"Of course it is," he said, squeezing her hand. "I'm sorry."

"Yeah. Thanks." The fist that had closed around her throat relaxed, and she let out her breath on a sigh.

They sat together in silence until one of the football players came barreling their direction, running backward as he kept his eyes on the ball. He was a boy of eight or nine, thin and wiry, with dark black hair cut short and a ragged-looking shirt and shorts. Brit jumped up and caught the ball as it headed straight for Tori's head.

"Sorry," the boy said.

Brit sent the ball in a perfect spiral toward the group, who were now clumped in a group on the far side of the clearing.

The boy's eyes widened as the ball sailed easily through the air. "Wow. I wish I could throw like that."

"It takes practice," Brit said. "You can learn. What's your name?"

"Henry."

"You boys want a few pointers?"

Henry nodded vigorously, but pointed doubtfully at Brit's clothes. "My dad says he can't play when he's dressed for work."

"You boys promise not to tackle me, and we'll be fine."

With a wink to Tori, Brit sauntered over to the gaggle of kids. They looked away nervously as he approached, but their faces cleared when Brit held out a hand for the ball and began to demonstrate his throwing technique.

Tori watched with a sinking heart.

He was supposed to be Brit Bencher The Slayer, not Brit Bencher the good-with-kids-family-man who loved strong women and sacrificed his own dreams to take care of his family. He was not supposed to understand about her mother. She should never have told him about her mother. They were spending one night together. No strings, no attachment. She was not in the market for a relationship and neither was he.

Under Brit's watchful eye, the boys began to throw the ball back and forth among one another. After a few tries, the boy with the black hair threw the ball high into the air, where it formed an unsteady but distinct spiral, and then fell into the receiver's arms. Everyone cheered, even Tori. Brit looked over with a grin, dropped a million-dollar wink, and then turned back to the game.

Tori's heart fell right down into her toes. Her nails bit into her palm as she came to an unpleasant realization.

She could fall for him.

Damn it, she could fall for Brit Bencher.

Tori pulled out her BlackBerry and flipped through her messages at a furious clip. It was Friday evening and for once, she had nothing pressing to which she needed to respond. Instead, she dialed Betsy's home number.

"Hello?"

"Betsy, this is Tori. Listen, I'm so sorry to call you at home, but I have some good news." Helplessly, Tori let her gaze drift back to Brit, who was leaning over to assist one of the smaller boys with the football.

"Tori? Hold on a sec." Betsy screamed something at her kids that sounded suspiciously like a threat to tie them up and put them in a closet if they weren't quiet. A moment later, there was silence. "Okay, I've got about three minutes before they break something. What did you say? Something about good news? This has to do with The Slayer, doesn't it? Are you finally taking my advice?"

Tori bit her lip as Brit engineered another decent pass from a tiny kid who looked like he couldn't be more than seven years old. "I respectfully decline to answer the question," she said. "But I am staying in New York a couple of nights. So you don't have to go in to the office tomorrow morning. At least, you don't have to on my account. Feel free to go in if you like. But I won't be there."

Betsy let out a whoop that was loud enough to startle a duck that had wandered too close to Brit's jacket. In the background, Tori heard her yell, "I don't have to work tomorrow, kids! I can come to the game!"

The sound made Tori feel like dirt. "Jesus, Betsy, why didn't you tell me you had other plans? I could have found someone else to help me."

With a note of obvious relief, Betsy replied, "As if I'd let anyone else work on that presentation for Karl? Not a chance. But now that you're having a weekend of crazy sex with the hottest guy in NYC, I don't mind saying that we had tickets to a Phillies game and my sister was going in my place. Do you need me to change your reservations? I'd be more than happy to—I can do that from home, even."

Tori shifted uncomfortably on her jacket. "I didn't say we were…er…"

"Oh, don't be ridiculous. I know exactly what's going on there." Tori could picture Betsy's airy wave of her hand, and the knowing look in her eyes. "Listen, if he has mirrors on the ceiling, I want to know about it."

"Betsy!" Tori looked back at Brit, who was headed her direction. "Don't worry about my ticket, I'll take care of it. You're the best. And tell me next time you've got something going on over the weekend, okay?"

Betsy's voice turned serious. "You may be a demanding workaholic, but you're also the best boss I've ever had. The game wasn't a big deal. I'd have told you if it was. I'm glad you're staying. You need this."

Tori found her attention slowly slipping away as Brit approached. He had unbuttoned his top button, exposing smooth olive skin that begged to be touched.

"Anything else I should know about?" She tried for calm. "Any emergencies in the office?"

Betsy snorted. "Oh please. If there's an emergency, you'll probably hear about it on that damn BlackBerry before I get wind of it. You go run off and enjoy your weekend of naughtiness. It isn't as though you haven't earned it."

"Yeah, right," Tori said. "I'll see you on Monday."

"Bye."

Betsy started hollering at her kids before she hung up the phone. Tori slipped her phone into her purse, her gaze lingering on the deep V of his shirt.

"Trouble at home?" Brit asked.

She forced her gaze back to his face. His eyes crinkled at the corners, and a faint sheen of perspiration glistened on his forehead. "Actually, I made someone very happy. My assistant was going to have to work tomorrow, and now she doesn't." She forced the words over her suddenly inarticulate tongue.

"That should get you a card on Boss's Day." Brit offered his hand. "We should probably head back. They don't like it when you're late at the helipad."

"Are we still going through with that?"

"Absolutely. You don't like heights, remember? I'm hoping you'll be terrified and have to fling yourself into my arms for comfort."

She snorted. "Sorry. I, er, exaggerated. I used to go rock climbing with friends in college. I'm not really scared of heights."

He grabbed his jacket from the ground and shook it out with a *snap*. "That sounds like a challenge. What's the penalty?"

"For what?" She peeled her coat from the flattened grass.

"If you're wrong. If you're grabbing my hand and saying your prayers when we take off."

They walked back to the paved path and started for the car. He extended his hand to join hers and they fell into a natural rhythm. His touch sent a warm shiver from her palm to her stomach, and then down to her toes.

"How would you know?" she asked. "What's to stop me from lying?"

"Oh, you won't lie," he said. "And if you do, I'll know. I've seen your poker face, remember?"

Tori kicked a stick from the path, feeling almost giddy with pleasure at the very presence of the man by her side. She considered her options.

"I've got an idea." She leaned over and whispered into his ear.

He nodded approvingly. "Sounds acceptable."

"What about you? What if I take one look at your puny helicopter and laugh in the face of danger?"

"First of all, never insult the size of a man's helicopter. Second, that's not the terms of the bet. I've seen you in action, remember? You're already tough as nails. You probably laugh in the face of danger five times a day. We're talking about grabbing my hand."

His words had the odd effect of silencing the girlish pleasure that had been running through her veins. *Tough as nails*. That's what everyone thought about her. The doctors at Langston Estates would say, "Some families don't want these sort of details, but we thought you would, Ms. Anderson." Her partners joked about giving her the most difficult clients.

"Tori can handle him," they'd say. "She's a tough nut herself."

No wonder Phil dumped me. Who wanted to date a tough nut?

"I see."

"Hey, that was a joke." He peered over at her. "Haven't I already paid your forfeit today?"

She forced a smile. "I suppose you have."

"Well then, I suppose I have nothing to lose."

He had nothing to lose. Tori only wished she could say the same for herself.

Chapter Ten

An hour later, Tori got the first inkling that she was going to owe Brit a special favor later that night. At least when she'd been rock climbing, she'd been attached to a rope. This was entirely different. They were surrounded by plastic, in a tiny bubble that seemed entirely too transparent for comfort. The seat belt seemed marginal as their only piece of safety equipment. Shouldn't they be wearing parachutes? Or at least a full body harness?

The blades of the chopper made a whumping sound as they started up, gradually going faster and faster, until the noise turned into one loud whine, not unlike being in the very back row of a 747 when it was taking off—times ten.

Brit grinned as Tori slipped the wide earphones over her head. They instantly canceled the background noise, and she was surrounded by the smooth sound of Miles Davis's *Kind of Blue*. Brit's voice sounded over the music, oddly intimate even though she couldn't hear it from his lips.

"I ordered us some mood music. Are you feeling all right? You're looking pale," he said.

The seats were surprisingly comfortable, smooth leather, with a padded headrest and cradle surrounding her upper body. They were squeezed in shoulder to shoulder, her knees inches from the back of the pilot's seat.

"I'm fine," she said, swallowing hard.

"Don't worry, most people have a moment of panic before they lift off," Brit said. He held out his hand. "Do you want to squeeze my hand? It might make you feel better."

His eyes were twinkling with mischief. Tori kept her hands in her lap. She'd been set up. He knew this would happen.

"Welcome to the tour, Ms. Anderson, Mr. Bencher." The pilot's voice came over the headphones.

He sounded confident. Tori appreciated that confidence. She only wished he didn't look like a twenty-year-old college kid. There was an age requirement for pilots, wasn't there?

"We'll begin by flying down the Hudson River to New York's harbor. From there, we'll take a close-up look at Ms. Liberty and Ellis Island, and then turn toward the Verrazano Bridge. On the way back up the river, we'll take you past the Financial District and the Empire State Building."

Tori took deep, calming breaths. She had never been scared of heights before. What was wrong with her?

"It's a combination of the small quarters, the loss of control, and the unfamiliar feeling of a vertical takeoff," Brit said, reading her mind. "Really, it's okay. You can squeeze hard, I won't mind."

He held out his hand again. Tori ignored it and formed her own into a fist.

"You're not going to take my hand, are you?" Brit said.

"When we start falling from the sky in a death spiral, and not a moment before."

"Would it kill you to show some weakness?"

Tori turned to glare at him. "I can be weak," she said,

tightening her jaw as the helicopter lurched the first few feet off the ground. As the ground receded below, she swallowed hard and tried not to panic. "At the right time. For a very good reason." She tried not to look out the window. "Do they have those bags in helicopters? You know, the ones they put on the planes? The waterproof ones?"

"You're thinking too much again," Brit chided. "You're forcing me to take drastic steps. Now hold still, this is for your own good."

He leaned over and kissed her.

Too surprised to put up a fight, Tori let him kiss the butterflies from her stomach. By the time he pulled away, she realized she had grabbed his hand and was holding on as if her life depended on it.

"Now look," he said, and pointed out the clear plastic windows that surrounded them.

Still dazed from the perfect warmth of his lips, Tori finally looked outside and caught her breath on a gasp. The dark creep of the Hudson River seemed only inches below as they swooped through the clear skies, the buildings laid out like tiny gray pieces in a model train set. It was truly like flying, so close to the ground yet captured and suspended above. Slowly, her fear dissolved and was replaced by a childlike wonder.

Loosening her grip on Brit's hand, Tori leaned forward to get a better view. As the poignant, evocative sound of Davis's trumpet washed over her, she became aware of the beauty of the city in a way she never had before. The blue sky met the horizon with its endless line of buildings, their windows catching the late afternoon sun in a sparkle of light. In the harbor, sailboats raced the wind, white-tipped stars in the dark waters. Ahead, she caught the spectacular sight of the Statue of Liberty, radiant in her green glow.

"Oh my," she gasped, as they approached the statue. The

face loomed in front of them, large and solemn, beautiful in her austerity.

"Isn't she something?" Brit said.

"It's…incredible," Tori said, unable to tear her gaze away. "The most incredible thing I've ever seen."

. . .

Later that night, Brit's driver dropped them off outside a tall building with dark gray stone steps leading to a porch surrounded by an elegant balustrade. A doorman appeared as they passed through the pool of light cast by an antique street lamp, and they were ushered into a warm lobby with a thick red carpet over a marble floor.

"Evening, Mr. Bencher," the doorman said.

"Evening, Seth," Brit said. "This is Tori Anderson. She's from Philly."

Seth, a slender, dark-skinned man with big ears and a wide smile, touched the top of his hat. "Ma'am," he said gravely, "I'm sorry to hear that."

"What's wrong with Philly?" Tori asked, trying not to care that Brit had made a point of introducing her to his doorman.

"Nothing six weeks of spring training, a new coach, and dozen or so new players couldn't cure." Seth grinned and revealed two gold teeth.

"Oh." Tori smiled, wishing she had something to offer back in the way of sports banter.

"Weather tomorrow calls for high of eighty-three. Should be perfect for Luke's game," Seth offered.

Brit smacked his forehead. "Luke's game, how could I have forgotten?" He turned to Tori. "I hope you don't mind catching a Little League game tomorrow. Luke wouldn't let me live it down if I missed it. I'm sure he'd love to have you there."

"Little League?" Tori said doubtfully. Brit wanted her to go to his nephew's baseball game? That seemed out of character for a weekend of no-strings-attached sexual bliss.

"As long as you don't mind," Brit said.

Tori flipped through possible explanations for the invitation and settled on one almost immediately: Brit was simply trying to be polite. He could hardly ask her to stay at his place while he went to the game without her. Not after he'd gone out of his way to convince her to stay for the weekend.

She pondered the appropriate response.

Work. That would do the trick. She gave him a bright smile. "I don't mind staying here. I have some reading I need to do."

He frowned. "I thought this was a no-work weekend."

What did that mean? He sounded genuinely irritated by her response. "I thought..." Why would he want her to meet his family? She racked her brain for an explanation for Brit's response but found none. "Well...I guess I could come. I don't want to hurt Luke's feelings."

"Great." He pushed her in the direction of the elevators, pausing a moment to wave at the doorman. "Thanks for the reminder, Seth."

"No problem, Mr. Bencher. Nice to meet you, Miss Anderson."

Tori waved to Seth as the elevator doors opened. Once inside, the silence had a disturbing intimacy. The whole night had been like this—periods of lighthearted flirtation followed by unexpected closeness, as if they were two people embarking on something very different from her promised one-night stand.

She flipped through her repertoire of conversation topics, determined to get back on track for a weekend of unemotional, physical release. If she wasn't careful, the next thing to emerge from her lips would be some confession about her mother, or a complaint about the pressures of applying for partnership. Yuck. But what did a fun, sexy, not-obsessed-with-her-job woman talk about? Her typical conversation gambits were suitable for conferences, law firm dinners, and client lunches. None seemed to fit the "fun and sexy" profile.

She thought about Betsy and her talk of the Phillies, and then Harold's comment in the lobby. That was it! Sports. Cute women always knew something about sports. That was why guys fell for them—they could actually speak the same language.

"So, what position does Luke play?" Immediately, she panicked. They had positions in baseball, right?

"Right field."

"Oh, he must be very good then. Right field, wow." She put a hand on her hip and tried to look cool and knowledgeable.

"Tori," Brit said, "right field is a terrible position. The only kids who hit to right field are left-handed batters."

"And there aren't many of those, I gather?" Cool and knowledgeable slipped through her fingers.

"Not very." His lips twitched. "You're a big sports fan, I take it?"

Tori waved an airy hand. "Oh yeah, sports. Love 'em. Can't get enough of football, that's for sure." She thought again of Betsy. "And the Phillies. Die-hard Phillies fan, that's me."

He grabbed her hand and pulled her against him. When he was looking down into her eyes, he chuckled and stole a quick kiss. "Do you even know what sport the Phillies play?"

Tori considered the options. It was almost summer. Wasn't baseball a summery sport? "Baseball, of course," she said confidently.

Never let them see you sweat. Tori's Rules of Negotiation Number Five.

He slid his hand across her cheek. "Lucky guess."

They reached the top floor and the elevator doors opened to a quiet hallway with an oriental runner in shades of burgundy and gold. The door at the end of the hall had a stained glass insert and a curved bronze handle. Brit opened the lock and pulled her inside.

"Are you a golf fan?" she asked. "I can talk about golf."

"What is it with lawyers and golf?" Brit mused. He hung up his coat and then spun her around. The back of her suit still had an assortment of stains and spots of mud. "You should have sat on my jacket."

"I have others. But about your golf game—where do you like to play?"

"I don't play golf." He took her hand and led her through an expansive entryway, past a dining area with an enormous table that had seats for twelve and a gleaming kitchen with stainless steel appliances and granite countertops, and then down another hall to a large room at the end. He hit a switch and the lights turned on, revealing a mahogany king-size bed, abstract images on the walls in shades of orange, brown, and red, and heavy, masculine furniture. A bank of windows looked out over a city of blinking lights.

The room smelled of Brit. It turned her insides cold, then hot. He dropped his coat on a chair, then began methodically unbuttoning his shirt.

"Really?" she asked, unable to move or tear her eyes away from his strongly muscled torso. "I thought every executive played golf."

"Golf," he said slowly, dropping the shirt on top of the jacket, "is for wimps. And lawyers."

"Oh. I see."

He pulled off his belt, and added it to the pile. Kicked off his shoes. Her mouth went dry.

"I don't play golf," she said, her jacket falling from her shoulders onto the ground. She leaned over and pulled off her heels, and set them by a dresser. Her body moved mechanically, her eyes pinned on the man in front of her who was rapidly becoming nude. "Never learned. It's not as easy as it looks. Men definitely have an advantage."

"How so?" He moved behind her and tugged on the zipper of her skirt. It fell to the floor in a soft rustle. Brit offered one hand and Tori took it as she stepped out of the garment.

"Breasts," she said huskily, her voice catching as soon as she caught sight of his naked form. Lord, he was like a statue, dark hair in a fine mat on his chest, sinewy muscles, and hard lines.

"What's wrong with breasts?" He cupped hers, following the lacy edges of bra to a front clasp that he opened with a flick of his fingers. "I like breasts. Yours in particular. They're the perfect size," he said as he pushed the bra to the ground and captured their weight in his hands, "and the perfect shape." He leaned forward to kiss each nipple.

Tori's head fell back as soon as his lips touched her. She paused by the side of the bed, unable to move or think as he replaced his lips with his tongue.

"They get in the way," she finally managed to say.

"These breasts?" He looked at them, incredulous. "These breasts could never be in the way. Shame on you for suggesting such a thing. Now this thong, on the other hand..." He motioned toward it with a mocking grin. "This thong is absolutely unnecessary."

Tori looked down. He was right. She slid off the thong.

She started to lower herself to the bed, but Brit caught her around the waist.

"Hold on," he said. Jumping onto the bed in front of her, he arranged himself carefully in the middle of the comforter. With a wicked smile, he patted the space next to him. "You do have a forfeit to pay, you recall. My hand definitely got squeezed."

Tori looked down at the beautiful male animal in front of her and smiled. "That's not the only thing that's going to get squeezed."

"Oh." he closed his eyes. "Be gentle. That's all I ask."

She lowered herself to the bed by his side. "Gentle, nothing. I'm the one paying the forfeit. Sometimes when I lose a bet I get a little," she kissed the side of his knee, "frustrated."

He made a strangled noise. "Frustrated?"

She brushed her mouth against his thigh. With firm hands, she pushed his legs apart to give herself more room. Straddling one leg, she slid her hands up, teasing herself with the touch of his wiry hair between her thighs, lingering at the edges of his sex with the barest scratch of her fingernails.

"I have a lot of energy. I need to release that energy somehow."

He sucked in a breath. "No argument here."

"I didn't think so." Her lips followed the path of her hands and she reveled in his quick, indrawn breath. This man made her feel so gloriously wanton, sexier than she'd ever been before. And she was going to enjoy every minute. She explored him slowly, refusing to hurry. The soft skin of his scrotum yielded easily to her touch, his penis leaping the moment she brushed against it with her hair.

"Mmmm," she sighed, cupping his balls in one hand as she ran her fingers over the length of him.

He touched her head with one hand, the gentle motion affirming his appreciation for her efforts. His soft skin pulsed under her fingers. Reveling in the desire already throbbing between her legs, Tori flicked her tongue around the head of his cock, lingering at the tiny scar at the base where he had been circumcised. Then, letting her teeth bump gently against him, she finally took him into her mouth, stopping for a moment to let him throb and harden even more. When he buried his other hand in her hair and urged her on, she let him slide the rest of the way into her mouth, until he reached the back of her throat.

Glorying in the feel of him, she sucked hard and moved her mouth up and down his length. When he moaned she felt an answering tug of desire and rode his thigh hard, grinding against him as she pulled and sucked deep, then retreated to run her tongue up and down the dark, throbbing vein.

She tasted a sweet, salty flavor as he bucked against her and retreated, took one of her breasts in her hand, and rubbed the nipple against him instead. That, apparently, was all he could take, because his strong hands suddenly found their way to her waist.

"No more," he groaned, lifting her away from him.

Tori rolled onto her back. She realized that Brit was sheathing himself in a condom, and she whimpered as an unexpected wave of desire hit her. He touched her gently, his long fingers probing her as if to make sure she was ready. She spread her thighs and moved her hips, suddenly desperate to feel him deep inside.

Brit drove into Tori with hard, powerful thrusts that seemed to reach her very core. The tension in her built to a second, equally powerful crescendo, and she pulled back her legs to welcome him as deeply as possible. Brit took one of her knees in his hand and pushed it higher, toward her shoulder, leaning into her as he thrust. Feeling vulnerable and powerful at the same time, Tori moved against him, rising to meet his thrusts. When the moment of surrender came she let it overwhelm her body and mind, and screamed at the pleasure, dizzy with the force of her release. Seconds later, Brit uttered a hoarse cry, buried his face in her neck, and shuddered to stillness.

Chapter Eleven

Tori awoke to the sound of Brit's heavy breathing, the warmth of an arm flung over her shoulder, and the urgent press of her bladder. With cautious fingers, she peeled Brit's arm off her body and squirmed her way out of the covers. Tori smothered a groan as she pushed herself to standing, and then looked around the room for something to wear. She had intended to be back home last night, and hadn't brought anything with her other than her briefcase and the clothes on her back.

"You aren't running away, are you?" came a gravelly voice. Brit had opened one eye, and was considering her in a hazy, unfocused sort of way.

"No. I need a bathroom."

"First door on the left. You better be here when I wake up."

He closed the eye and resumed snoring a moment later. Hopping around the house naked didn't sound appealing, so Tori examined her clothes. Strewn about the room were her silk shirt, skirt, and thong. Not exactly the sort of outfit she was looking for.

Feeling a bit like a thief, she padded quietly over to the imposing, dark mahogany unit across from the bed. She pulled the top drawer open and found neatly folded boxer briefs and carefully matched socks. The next two drawers held perfectly arranged white undershirts. The fourth drawer had colored T-shirts, sorted by shade, and the fifth, a collection of wrinkleless gym shorts. Unless he was obsessive-compulsive, Brit neither did his own laundry nor put it away.

She looked back over to the man stretched out at an angle on the bed, mouth open as he snored, hair a tousled mess. No, she smiled, definitely not obsessive-compulsive. Rich, but not compulsive.

She pulled out a blue T-shirt and slipped it over her head, and then found a pair of cotton shorts that hung low on her hips, but didn't fall off. The scent of sandalwood tickled her nose, and she buried her face in the shirt for a moment. Though she no longer had any excuse, she continued her stealthy examination. An open door to the left revealed a walk-in closet, with rows of suits, shirts, and pants, all hung on identical hangers approximately an inch apart. Neat birch shelves held a collection of sweaters and polos.

Was it wrong to envy a man for his closet? Or perhaps simply for the maid and laundry service that kept it so well organized?

She backed out of the closet and headed out the door to find the bathroom. After relieving her very full bladder—and examining another impeccably cleaned and organized room—she continued down the hall toward the kitchen. Along the way she stopped at the open door of what appeared to be Brit's office. Looking around guiltily, she stepped across the threshold, clasping her arms around her like a cloak.

Once inside, she took in the appearance of the room with wide-eyed approval. The rest of the house smacked of some vaguely pretentious, wealthy yuppie who didn't like kids, messes, or clutter. But this room was different. This room was Brit.

She slid her index finger along the edge of a 1950s-style walnut desk and was enormously relieved to find a trail of dust. The desk held an assortment of papers, reports, open books, and even a few half-empty coffee cups. A laptop sat on a table opposite the desk, surrounded by more papers. On one wall hung a framed poster of Sean Connery in *Goldfinger*. Another wall held a picture of the New York skyline that Tori guessed had been taken from a helicopter. A series of black and white photographs of children decorated the space by the door—nieces and nephews, perhaps. Under a tall window sat a glass box with a baseball inside. A close examination revealed the name Roger something—Earis? Waris?—scrawled across the ball.

Tori nibbled her lip as she stared at the ball. Maris! Roger Maris. That was it. She congratulated herself for coming up with the name. She wasn't entirely sure where she'd heard it, but she suspected, based on the programs sitting on top of the case, that he played for the Yankees. She'd have to Google him when she got home. Brit would be impressed when she—

In the middle of the thought, she smacked herself on the forehead and backed away from the case as if it were radioactive. Once she got home, she was never going to have anything to do with Brit Bencher ever again. How could she have forgotten?

She hurried out of the study and made a beeline for the kitchen.

This is a one-night—no, make that two-night—stand. He's out of your league, dates women for nanoseconds, enjoys the company of supermodels, and is absolutely not interested in a relationship, and neither are you.

And she was okay with that.

She found the kitchen, which even Martha Stewart

couldn't complain about, and started rifling through glass-doored cabinets. She needed coffee. Now. This very instant. Dark, strong, bitter coffee that would restore the mental faculties that had apparently been melted away by Brit's smoldering kisses.

Remember Fritzy? The damn cat who abandoned you? You can't even keep an animal happy, let alone another human being. Brit is heartache in a pretty wrapper. Enjoy this weekend for what it is—rampant sexual pleasure with no emotional ties.

"Third cabinet to the left for the beans. The grinder's next to the sink."

She jumped at the sound of a voice and spun around. Long and lean, Brit stood behind her, his sculpted torso bare, a pair of striped cotton pajama bottoms covering his lower half.

"Thanks. I'm useless until I get that first cup." *Play it cool,* she warned herself. *Remember, no emotions. No emotions...*

"Depends on how you define useless." He wagged an eyebrow at her outfit. "You look like you're ready to shoot some hoops. There's big bucks in that, you know."

She allowed herself to laugh. Laughing wasn't emotional, was it? "Hoops? I assume that means basketball?"

He gave a long-suffering sigh. "I can see this is going to be a problem. I can accept that you never played any sports yourself, but didn't you say you were engaged once? I assume that was to a man, right?"

"I suppose you could call him that."

"Clearly, not man enough."

A wide smile broke across her face. "Phil was, well...he played a lot of golf."

Brit nodded sagely. "I knew it. Obviously, his leaving was for the best."

Talking about her ex-fiancé this way was highly enjoyable,

but risked becoming emotional, so Tori decided to change the subject. "So, what about those pancakes you were talking about? Does a girl have to starve around here?"

He put his hands on his hips. "No one is going to be doing any starving. Not on my watch. The flour is in the corner cabinet. You can be my sous chef."

"You actually use this kitchen?" Tori turned to open the cabinet and found a revolving lazy Susan filled with neat glass containers. She pulled out the one that said "FLOUR" and set it on the counter. "I thought maybe you had a full-time maid and cook."

"Why would you assume I'm helpless? Are you a sexist, Tori Anderson?"

Brit opened a drawer in the wide, granite-topped island in the center of the room. He pulled out a stack of recipe cards and flipped through them. Setting one dog-eared index card on the counter, he threw the others back in the drawer, and closed it.

"Yes, I am a sexist, but no, that's not why I assumed you are helpless. Using my keen lawyer's brain, I deduced that were you actually a functioning chef, there would at least one coffee stain on the coffeemaker, a scratch on the snowy-white sink, or a spot on the counter. Seeing none of those things, I assumed not much cooking gets done in here."

He hummed as he moved around the kitchen. Tori leaned against the counter and watched as he pulled buttermilk and an egg from the enormous Sub-Zero fridge. The muscles in his back flexed and rippled.

"We will come back to your sexism in a moment. But in answer to your question, I have a very good cleaning service."

Tori wrinkled her nose. "Cleaning service, laundry service…you had someone come in here and organize your closet, too, didn't you?"

"Maybe. Does that bother you? I need the sugar, baking

soda, salt, and baking powder, by the way." He had pulled out a large mixing bowl and measuring cups from the cabinet under the island and began to scoop out the flour.

"It's a touch, well, *sterile* in here, don't you think?"

"Most women like it."

"Who's being sexist now? Are you suggesting that women are shallow creatures who like your sterile apartment because it shows off how rich you are?" She found baking soda and powder and added them to the counter.

"I said nothing of the sort. Unlike you, I am not a sexist. My sister, Melissa, organized this place for me. She said I wasn't using my space very well. My brother Joe's wife, Allison, did the decorating. The women I know seem to like things that are organized and decorated. And frankly, I spend my time in my office, unless I'm entertaining, so I don't really care what the rest of the house looks like."

Great, now she had managed to insult both his sister and sister-in-law. Still, he looked more amused than annoyed. "Sorry about that," she said. "I didn't know your sisters had done the decorating. I happened to notice that your office is the only thing in this house that looks like you. That's all."

He raised an eyebrow. "You don't think I'm—how did you put it—sterile?"

"I suppose *tidy* would be a better word."

A smile broke across his face. "You don't think I'm tidy?"

Tori spun the lazy Susan until she found the salt and set it down on the counter with a thump, suddenly annoyed with the conversation and her reaction to it. Brit was too damn charming and she was enjoying this banter far too much. She had to put a stop to it. "I have no idea if you're tidy or not. Forget I mentioned it."

"So now I'm helpless and untidy. And this after one date." He rustled through the contents of another drawer until he found measuring spoons.

"Dinner," she corrected him. "Sex. No dates. We're not dating, remember?"

It had become crucially important to remind herself of that fact. They were not dating.

"Of course," he agreed. "We are not dating."

"As long as we're clear about that." Tori cleared her throat, and turned around to retrieve the sugar. He could tease her all she wanted. She was getting out of this weekend with her sanity and dignity intact. Even if she had to die trying.

• • •

Brit carefully measured the ingredients and handed them back to Tori. He watched out of the corner of his eye as she put them away. When she reached up, the soft knit fabric of the shorts outlined her round bottom, and he felt a tug at his groin. He should be exhausted after that incredible night, but having her only seemed to make him want her more.

When he first set out to convince Tori to give him Solen's number, he never guessed how enjoyable that task would be. He had imagined a slightly unpleasant night of trying to create sympathy in the heart of a barracuda. Instead, he found a sexy, funny, tough-on-the-outside woman with a painfully obvious vulnerability underneath.

Whoa there, cowboy. Keep talking like that and people will think you like her.

Brit forced himself to shrug off the moment, as if the thought hadn't hit him somewhere between the gut and the solar plexus.

So what if I do like her? I like her breasts, her legs, her mouth...what's wrong with that? Besides, she doesn't want to date me any more than I want to date her.

Strangely enough, her insistence on treating this like a one-night stand irritated him. What was wrong with dating him? He wasn't malformed, old, or poor. He didn't have a wart on the end of his nose or an unfortunate habit of burping at dinner. They had shared a night of mind-blowing sex. There were legions of women who would be ecstatic at the thought of dating Brit Bencher. What made her so special?

He turned to the stove and prepared the griddle. He had put aside any thought of Melissa and Solen last night, but he couldn't ignore his task forever. Today would be the day. He'd do it subtly, and cleverly. He'd get her to fall in love with Melissa. He'd get her to *want* to give him the phone number.

Tori opened the cabinet with the coffee beans and threw some in the grinder. She pushed the button and filled the kitchen with noise, her face relishing the physical act of pulverizing the beans. Her mood had changed again. Was she pissed that he'd mentioned dating? Did she not like pancakes? It was hard to say, but he found it fascinating to watch the emotions flit across her face.

When the crunch of the grinder turned to a softer whir, he took it gently from her hands. "I think they're done. Why don't you let me handle this? You can get the newspaper. It should be at the front door by now."

Without a word, she marched out of the kitchen and over to the front door. After playing for a moment with the locks, she opened the door and retrieved the *Wall Street Journal*. She stalked back over to the dining room table and buried her face in the newsprint.

After starting the coffee, Brit turned to the griddle, glancing back at Tori every few seconds. It seemed risky, given her current mood, but if he was going to win her sympathy, he needed to start laying it on.

He decided to begin by talking about the kids. Women loved kids. She'd never notice when he turned to Melissa.

"My nephew Luke will be thrilled to have another spectator at his game. He's always complaining that no one comes to watch him."

"Is that right?" Tori did not lower the paper.

He stopped in the midst of picking up the pancake bowl, nonplussed by her chilly reaction. "Yes." There was a long pause. He wondered how to move the conversation forward. "Luke's nine," he finally threw out.

"That's nice."

He stared at the back of her head. She turned the page, folding the newspaper into neat thirds so it was easier to read.

"He's got a brother, Matt, and a baby sister, Julia. And then there's Delia, my brother Joe's kid. She's a handful, but so cute you can't bring yourself to get mad at her."

"They sound sweet. Is that coffee ready yet?"

Brit started getting annoyed. What kind of woman didn't start ooh-ing and aah-ing over a man's nieces and nephews? Wasn't that like the Holy Grail of dating? Despite all her assurances that she didn't want a relationship, surely she couldn't resist the chance to meet his family.

"No, it's not." Succumbing to his growing frustration, Brit started looking for a way to goad her into a reaction. "Luke's a bit of a bookworm, but generally a good kid. Not much of a ballplayer, but he'll learn. As long as we can keep his nose in the game and out of his books this summer."

"What's wrong with being a bookworm?" She dropped the paper and glared at him. "You have a problem with reading?"

Bingo.

"No, no problem," he said, pouring out four perfect dollar-sized pancakes. "But not over the summer. Kids are supposed to play sports over the summer, not read."

"Maybe he doesn't like sports. Maybe you should let him read." Her chin thrust forward.

"Everyone knows too much reading isn't good for a kid. Stunts their growth."

"Why that's the stupidest—" Her face started to go red, then abruptly she let out a long breath. "You're teasing me, aren't you?"

"Good heavens, no," he said with a straight face. "Why would I do a thing like that?"

"Hmph." She picked up the paper and buried her face behind it.

Brit flipped four golden pancakes, waited for the coffee to finish brewing, and then grabbed plates and cups. He poured a cup of coffee and brought it to Tori. "Sugar and cream?"

"No."

"You're sure? It might improve your mood."

She scowled at him. "Your stock closed down a buck yesterday."

He shrugged. "Markets move. Anything else interesting going on in the world? What are Jennifer and Brad up to these days?"

"I hardly think they cover that in the *Wall Street Journal*. Besides, it's been Brad and Angelina for years. They have like eight kids. Don't you know anything?"

"Drink your coffee," he advised. "I'll bring you the sugar."

Gathering the first batch of pancakes in one hand, and maple syrup, a sugar bowl, and two forks in another, he returned to the table. He set the plate in front of her with a flourish. Her eyes widened when she saw the pancakes.

"My God, these look amazing." Without even waiting for him to unload his arms, she popped one into her mouth. "Ahhh." She leaned back in the chair. "Now that's a pancake. Smooth and light, the tangy finish of the buttermilk." She took a sip of her coffee. "And a dark roast to go with them." A smile of contentment broke across her lips.

"So that's it," Brit said, setting down the syrup, forks, and sugar.

"What?" She picked up another pancake and ate it before he could respond.

"You're like the polar bear at the zoo. You get grumpy with your handler when you're hungry. I'll remember that."

She poured maple syrup over the pancakes, cut one in half with the fork, and ate it in a single bite. "Honey, with pancakes like these, you can handle me any day."

"Now that's more like it." He leaned forward to lick a drop of syrup from her lips. "Mmm. Tastes good."

"Don't you have more pancakes to cook?" She gave him a suspicious eye.

He snapped back to his full height, and gave her a mock salute. "Yes, sir." She was moodier than a three-year-old on a sugar high, but for some reason he found himself enjoying it. He couldn't remember the last time a woman had been so grumpy with him—or the last time he'd made someone pancakes. The women he dated were more of the "coffee and cigarettes for breakfast" type.

He cooked the rest of the pancakes while she read the paper. He watched her methodical progress—first the business section, then the front page, then the national news. He joined her as she was leaning back in her chair, her hands splayed on her stomach.

"How's the polar bear now?" he teased. "I'm not going to lose an eye if I get too close, am I?"

She closed her eyes. "Probably not. Those cakes were damn good."

"Thank goodness. Luke won't be happy if his uncle has to come to the game with only one eye. What if I miss the one fly ball to right field he's ever caught?"

"Is he really that bad?"

He drenched his pancakes with syrup and tucked in. "No. But in comparison with Matt, it can feel that way."

"How old is Matt?"

Brit forced himself not to react to her first show of interest in the family. "Seven."

"Poor kids." When he looked at her quizzically, she said, "I mean, your brother mentioned at dinner the other night that he shares custody with his ex. It's tough to go through a divorce when you're that young."

"Ross and his wife got married out of high school. They were too young, never really got a chance to find themselves before they started having babies. They're both much happier now."

Tori nodded, but looked unconvinced.

"What?" he asked.

She shook her head. "Never mind. Forget it."

"No, what? You have something against divorce?"

"I'm sorry. I don't mean to sound critical of your brother, but I know how hard it is on kids."

"Did your parents divorce?" he asked, realizing this was the first time she'd voluntarily shared something about herself with him.

"My dad took off when I was eight. My mom never really recovered. I spent a lot of time blaming myself for him leaving, and then blaming her for scaring him away." Her voice drifted off, and a look of panic crossed her face, as if she had said something she shouldn't. She cleared her throat and made an obvious attempt to change the subject. "So what's Delia like?"

Reluctantly, he let her have her way, feeling as though he'd had his first glimpse into what made Tori the driven, ambitious person that she was. "Delia turned three a few weeks ago, but you'd think she was thirteen, considering the way she has everyone wrapped around her finger. She's a competitive bugger, too. She reminds me of Melissa, actually."

"Melissa's your sister, right?" She leaned forward in her chair.

Nice segue, Brit, he thought smugly. "That's right. I forgot I had mentioned her. She went to MIT and majored in computer science, then went right on to a master's degree. She's always been one of the only women in her classes, but it doesn't seem to bother her. She shrugs it off and keeps right on going."

"She must be tough," Tori said, nodding approvingly.

"Yes, but I worry about her. She's so independent, she refuses to let me get involved, but she's been such a mess since—" Brit cautioned himself not to look Tori directly in the eye as he dropped the hook into the water.

"Since she broke up with her boyfriend?"

A bite!

"Well, I'm not sure I should talk about it. She's fairly private about these sorts of things."

"Oh, of course." Tori stood up and brought her plate and cup into the kitchen. "I didn't mean to pry. I should probably take a shower. What time is the game?"

Damn it. "We've got plenty of time. Have another cup of coffee." As Tori poured, Brit continued, "The thing is, he cheated on her. With her best friend."

Tori spun around, her mouth dropping open. "Why, that's horrible! The bastard."

Brit did not need to fake his frustration. "Oh, he's a bastard all right. And I promise you, if he ever steps foot in this state, there will be hell to pay. But there's nothing I've been able to do for her. She's so depressed."

"My mom was like that," Tori said. "After my dad left. It took her months to pull herself back together."

Brit barely heard her words, as success loomed within his reach.

Bring it home, Brit!

"She spends all day wandering around, looking miserable," he pressed. "Half the time she won't even leave her apartment. I've tried everything to get her out of the house, but nothing seems to work. I think maybe if she got a job, she might be able to shake it."

Tori bit her lip. "You know, depression isn't necessarily something you can fix for someone else, Brit. Of course you want to get her help if she needs it, but she may not need you to intervene right now. She might need some time to work through it on her own."

Brit paused, momentarily distracted by her quiet words. Before any doubt could overcome him, he shook her voice from his head. He was going to help Melissa, and he was going to do it with Solen's number.

He stood and joined Tori by the sink, sliding his finger over the crease of her mouth before replacing it with his own lips.

"We've got half an hour," he breathed. "Let's forget all about my family and see if my polar bear still has her claws."

Chapter Twelve

The game started at eleven, so the sun was already hot overhead by the time Tori and Brit arrived at the ball field. The baseball diamond sat at one end of a neighborhood park in Brooklyn, near where Brit's brother Ross lived. Old oak trees ringed the park, casting cool shadows over a multicolored play structure, metal slide, and long row of swings. The grass was a thick emerald green, and neat rows of petunias and pansies decorated a flower bed at the entrance to the park. The air was humid, and even though the temperature wasn't much above seventy, Tori felt the prickle of sweat around her hairline as soon as they left the car.

It had occurred to both of them that Tori needed a new outfit for the game, so Brit stopped at a boutique not far from his apartment on their way out of Manhattan. Tori found a pair of black capri pants, strappy sandals, and a wildly overpriced T-shirt and convinced the clerk to let her wear them out of the changing room. She considered buying a hat as well, but since she'd already dropped enough on the shirt and pants to pay her mortgage for a few months, she decided to skip it, and dug an elastic out of her purse instead.

The way her heart was beating as they approached the stands, you would think she was back in high school. Except this time she wasn't nervous about talking to her crush, she was wondering how the hell she had ended up at a Little League game meeting his family.

"Uncle Brit!"

A small pack of children emerged from the bleachers as soon as Tori and Brit came into sight. Brit, looking painfully attractive in low-slung khakis and a dark gray polo shirt, broke into a wide smile.

"Hey, you rugrats!" he called out.

A small, black-haired girl reached them first, running as fast as she could on short, sturdy legs. Her face was tight with concentration, and she looked behind her several times, as if to make sure she was out in front. When she saw that her target was within reach, she squealed and threw herself forward in a flying leap. Brit scooped her up neatly right before she hit the ground, then flipped her upside down and tickled her belly before setting her gently into the grass. That was all the time necessary for the older kids to arrive. There was a tall, skinny boy in a baseball jersey, a younger boy wearing a pair of blue mesh basketball shorts, and a girl with chestnut pigtails, wearing matching pink shirt and shorts.

They all started talking at once, the smallest one, Delia, tugging on Brit's arm, the older ones trying to get his attention by speaking louder and louder. Tori recognized Ross, the brother she had met that first night at Alessandro's, as he waved from the stands.

She hung back, hoping to avoid making too much contact with the children. She loved kids, but this felt wrong. She was nobody, a woman whose relationship with Uncle Brit couldn't be—shouldn't be—explained. Worse yet was the thought that she'd have to look Brit's siblings in the eye. Would they be pitying? Embarrassed for her? Judgmental? They were real, adult people, and they were going to spoil her perfect fantasy world where she could have an affair with a fantastic guy, create no emotional baggage, and go home the next day and never think about him again.

"Hey, kids, this is Tori." Brit motioned for her to come closer. She did, reluctantly, and gave a tiny wave. They barely looked at her before resuming the chorus for Brit's attention.

Brit threw Delia back over his shoulder and began moving the party toward the bleachers. He admired the butterflies on Julia's shorts, gave Matt a high-five for getting the most rebounds in his basketball game the night before, and asked Luke if he was reading anything new.

They beamed at him, and began shouting answers in reply. All at once. Tori kept to the side and tried to make herself invisible.

It didn't work.

Ross jumped down from the metal bleachers and met Tori halfway. "As I live and breathe, it's Tori Anderson, right? From Alessandro's?" His considerable biceps strained the edges of an old T-shirt, and his grin could have melted an ice cube in thirty seconds flat.

Tori cringed at the amused look in his eyes. At least he wasn't looking at her as if she were a hooker. "That's me. It's Ross, right? Your kids are great."

"My kids are loud, ill-mannered, and completely in love with my brother." He shook his head at the sight of Brit, who was now casually flinging the shrieking Delia into the air, while still managing to carry on a conversation with Luke. "Brit mentioned he'd be bringing a friend to the game, but he didn't say it was you. It's nice to see you again."

A moment later, another man and a woman started toward them. The man was tall, with dark brown hair that slid over his forehead and wire-rimmed glasses in a messy wave. His clothing was nearly as disheveled, with a hopelessly wrinkled madras plaid shirt tucked haphazardly into a pair of faded canvas pants. Tori liked him immediately.

The woman, who Tori assumed was Melissa, had piercing blue eyes like her brother, and a thin, heart-shaped face with prominent cheekbones. A limp ponytail trailed down her back. She was too angular to be beautiful, though Tori could see she could have been striking had she not been quite so thin, or so clearly uninterested in her appearance.

Brit's words from the morning came back to her in a rush. No wonder he was so worried about her. Melissa looked like she was wasting away. It was heartbreaking, and Tori had only known her for a few minutes.

Brit suddenly appeared by Tori's side, the children still clinging to him like cheerful, screaming barnacles. "Joe, Melissa, this is a friend of mine—Tori Anderson. Tori, this is my brother Joe and sister, Melissa, and you remember Ross, from the restaurant."

Joe, whom Tori had already pegged as "the nice one" of the family, brushed his hair from his eyes and gave her a firm handshake. "Nice to meet you, Tori. You should know right away that Delia's a dangerous little cuss. Don't let her youth or innocence fool you."

The object of his announcement peered down from atop Brit's shoulders. "Daddy, what's dangerous mean?"

"You," Joe said, tickling her feet. She giggled appreciatively, and hugged the top of Brit's head tighter.

Tori laughed and nodded. "Thanks for the warning."

Melissa's gaze swept from Tori's toes to the top of her frizzy head. Her expression remained impassive, but Tori had the feeling everything about her had been analyzed and memorized in one penetrating look. "Nice to meet you. Are you new to the city?"

"No, I'm visiting," she said. "I live in Philly."

Ross smiled. "I met her a couple of weeks ago. At Alessandro's."

Melissa raised an eyebrow at Ross, who started to say something else before Brit cut him off abruptly. "Ross, Joe, why don't we take the kids and throw the ball around before the game starts?"

Matt and Julia cheered, while Luke looked marginally interested. Ross turned to Brit with a hurt look. "But I was getting acquainted with your friend Tori."

Her face already warm from the humidity and growing embarrassment, Tori waved her hand at him. "Please, don't worry about me. I was thinking about finding a spot in the shade until the game starts."

"Sounds like a good idea," Melissa agreed, though her face showed nary a flush. "I'll go with you."

Reluctantly, Ross nodded. He walked over to Brit and punched him in the arm as they walked toward the center of the field. Joe followed a few steps behind.

"Sometimes they're such...men," Melissa said, making no attempt to hide her bitterness.

"What's the old saying? Can't live with 'em, can't shoot 'em?" Tori said.

They began walking toward a large maple tree, its wide, spreading branches casting a pool of shadow over the edge of the ball field. Melissa stopped and raised an eyebrow. "You sure about that?"

Tori grimaced. Melissa's words dripped with sarcasm, but underlying it was an obvious, aching pain. Tori could understand why Brit wanted to kill the bastard who had cheated on his baby sister. "I suppose if you're careful enough..." she let her voice trail off suggestively.

The corner of Melissa's mouth twitched in the beginning of a smile. "Don't let Brit hear you say that."

"Oh, he'd understand," Tori said, waving a negligent

hand.

"So, how did you get mixed up with my brother, anyway?" Melissa asked, the smile disappearing as she stared out at the kids.

Tori paused, unsure what she was supposed to say. Brit had introduced her as a friend, which was not entirely true, but where was she supposed to go from there?

She recalled the way Brit had introduced her to Ross at Alessandro's, and decided to follow his lead. "We worked on a deal together."

"Really? I don't think Brit's ever met a...friend...that way." Melissa chose her words carefully.

Tori laced and unlaced her fingers. "You must follow your brother's friendships quite closely," she said, trying to keep her voice light. "To know that sort of detail, I mean."

Brit and his brothers had formed a rough triangle, with the kids in between. Every now and again, Ross or Joe would look curiously over at Tori, and she gritted her teeth. Brit remained focused on the children. He had the same look that he had when they were in Central Park: relaxed, comfortable, as much in control with a group of kids as he was in the boardroom.

"I'm sorry," Melissa said, "I don't mean to sound like a prude, but it's unusual for Brit to introduce us to someone. You must be very close?"

Tori crossed her arms over her chest. "We're not dating, if that's what you're asking. He didn't bring me here to meet the family. I probably got in the way and he was being polite." She smiled to try to make it sound playful, but knew she hadn't entirely disguised her frustration.

Why the hell am *I here?*

Melissa's eyebrows shot up at Tori's blunt response. She turned to face Tori and started to reply, but then apparently thought better of it, and closed her mouth. They stood for a moment in silence.

"I see," she said after a pause.

"I'm glad someone does," Tori said.

There was a brief commotion on the field as Luke got knocked in the shoulder by the ball. Tears ensued, though they dried up quickly as Matt teased him. Ross intervened, sending Matt to stand next to Joe and keeping Luke by his side.

"So, what do you do?" Melissa finally asked.

"I'm a lawyer," Tori replied.

"Is that right?" Melissa shot her a puzzled look. "A lawyer? Wow."

Tori stiffened. "What's so unusual about that?"

"Nothing." Melissa paused, then laughed before she continued, "I'm sorry, I think it's fabulous, actually. You see, Brit's taste usually runs toward a different sort of woman. A less, er…professional sort. If you know what I mean."

"Oh. Well, I'm also a cover model for *Vogue*. In my spare time," Tori added.

Melissa chuckled. "I don't mean to laugh, because you've got great legs, hon, but you'd need to add about a foot to each."

They shared a smile. "You're probably right. I shouldn't quit the day job. What about you?" Tori asked.

"I don't do anything," Melissa said, flipping her hair over her back. She stared at the kids in the field, but Tori had a sense she was seeing something else. "I used to work in a robotics lab with my Goddamn-cheating-bastard-ex-boyfriend. Now I sit through endless baseball games and listen to Brit tell me how I should move on and start over."

"I'm sorry," Tori said, struck by the raw pain in Melissa's voice.

"Yeah, not as sorry as I am."

. . .

As soon as this torture was over, Brit Bencher was a dead man. This was not the weekend she signed on for. If she wanted family drama, she could have stayed home and watched her mother slip into dementia.

She had wanted a weekend of no-drama sex. Apparently, Brit Bencher had something very different in mind.

Somewhere around the third inning, the pieces had begun to fall into place. Delia started it, when she pretended to do a robot dance for Auntie Melissa. Shortly after that, Joe asked Melissa if she'd made any progress on the job front.

Then Ross made a joke about Solen Labs, and how he doubted the place actually existed.

That was when Tori knew that she was being set up.

Brit was conveniently absent from her side for most of this time. If she didn't know better, she'd say he was making a concerted effort to leave her with Melissa while he roamed the field with the boys.

And, of course, now she did know better.

As the game progressed, Melissa filled in the details for Tori about her breakup with her boyfriend. She'd apparently caught him with his pants around his ankles, with her best friend. They were on the kitchen table. This explained why Melissa was so thin—she couldn't walk into a kitchen anymore without getting sick.

It was a horrible story, absolutely dreadful, and Tori couldn't help but feel sorry for Melissa, who seemed like a sweet person under her misery. She paid close attention to the kids on the field, and they seemed to look to her for approval. Everyone took turns competing to try to make her smile.

None of that made up for what Brit had tried to do.

She watched him on the field, a faint sheen of sweat glinting on his forehead, muscles rippling as he demonstrated a practice swing for Luke. He had that serious, patient look that made you want to trust him. Man or woman, no one was immune from that sort of cunning.

Yes, he was good, but Tori had seen the best in action. Her father, Thad, had been devilishly handsome. Unlike Brit, who worked the dark and sexy angle, Tori's father had a quick smile and roguish charm that women couldn't resist. Like her mother, Tori loved him fiercely, though she always doubted he loved her back.

After he left, she knew the truth.

Tori hadn't been surprised when he left. She'd always known she and her mother were too plain, too boring to keep her father's attention for long. It was her mother who never seemed to recover. Always reserved, Jeanne had simply grown colder over the years, as if she had given up on people completely.

Tori had never forgotten her father's lesson. And if Brit Bencher thought he was going to take her for a ride, he had another thing coming.

Chapter Thirteen

It was all Brit could do not to jump up and down as he watched Tori and Melissa talk during the rest of the game. He didn't understand what was going on with Tori—she refused to look him in the eye and kept scooting away from him on the bench. But he told himself that was irrelevant. What mattered was that his plan was working. Tori and Melissa had begun engaging in that mysterious female bonding that a wise man didn't try to understand. And once they did, there was no way Tori would be able to resist helping get Melissa a job.

He could barely retain a whoop of triumph.

Turning his attention to the field, Brit tried to pay attention to his nephew. He cheered at all the right times, gave the kid a thumbs-up sign when he walked off the field, and even went down to the bench along with Ross for a pep talk during the seventh-inning stretch. Yet throughout it all, Tori seemed to linger in the corner of his eye. Like a train wreck you try to ignore, but keep looking at through the rearview, Tori's bright halo of hair and wickedly intelligent eyes kept calling him. Even when he was talking to Luke, he found himself glancing up at her, watching the way her breasts moved when she wiped the sweat from her brow, or the sparkle in her eyes when she laughed at something Joe said.

"You've got it bad, don't you?" Ross chuckled over Luke's head. Like several of the other boys, by the seventh inning Luke was more interested in his drink box and snack than in any coaching. The two men drifted toward the trees and left the boys to their sugar-fest.

Brit ripped his gaze away from Tori's sweaty brow, briefly imagining the sheen of sweat that would cover her body later that night. He shook his head and tried to recall what his brother had said. "What's that?"

Ross laughed. "Exactly my point. Who is this girl?"

"A lawyer," Brit said.

"Not just any lawyer, apparently. Someone important enough to bring to Alessandro's, and now to Luke's game. Why haven't you said anything about her? Are you two serious?"

Brit winced. Somehow, in the midst of his planning and scheming, he hadn't considered what his family would think if he brought Tori to Luke's game. He was lucky Tori herself hadn't drawn any similar conclusion. "Good lord, no." He looked over his shoulder to make sure Melissa hadn't approached from behind and dropped his voice. "I'm hoping she can help Melissa. Without Melissa knowing."

Ross's eyes widened. "You're kidding. She's a…spy? A plant?"

"No, nothing like that! She happens to be the one person in the world who knows how to contact Garth Solen."

"*The* Garth Solen?" Ross rolled his eyes. "Good grief, didn't you do enough damage already by sending in Melissa's resume?"

Brit paused and scratched his arm. He couldn't quite meet his brother's eyes. "I don't know what you're talking about. Tori knows Solen, Melissa wants to work with Solen. I thought I should get them together."

"Without telling Melissa."

Brit nodded.

Ross blinked. "And for clarification—did you ask Tori out *before* or *after* you found out about her connection to Solen?"

"You're making this sound bad," Brit grumbled.

"I'm making this sound bad?" Ross said in disbelief. "You're leading Tori on, on the off-chance that she and Melissa will hit it off, and somehow she'll be able to get Melissa a job with Solen?" Ross shook his head. "That's bad, even for you."

"First of all, I don't need her to get Melissa a job. I need her to give me Solen's number."

"And then *you'll* get Melissa a job?"

"Melissa can get herself a job. I'm going to help break the ice. Besides, I'm not leading Tori on." Brit scowled. "In case you might have missed it, she's damned attractive. And she's not interested in anything serious. We're on the same wavelength."

"Hmm." Ross studied Brit. "You know, Melissa's a grown-up now. We all are. There's no reason for you to keep playing stand-in father."

"I am not your father," Brit said.

"I know that," Ross replied, "but sometimes I wonder if you do." He turned back to Tori, who was pulling her hair back from her face and laughing at something Joe was saying. "So you wouldn't mind if I asked her out?"

"Don't even think about it," Brit snapped, louder and angrier than he had intended.

"That's what I thought," Ross said.

"Wipe that smug look off your face. You've got three kids and an ex-wife to deal with. You don't need complications."

"She doesn't look complicated."

"Oh, she's complicated all right," Brit said. "This morning she jumped down my throat when I even suggested that we were dating. And I had to practically beg her to stay in New York overnight, even though it was perfectly obvious she wanted me." He was still mystified by her reluctance the day before. "I think she's a workaholic, on top of it. Checks her cell phone every ten minutes, even when we're at dinner. It's like a tic or something. I don't think she even knows she's doing it."

"That sounds terrible," Ross said with a straight face. "You're obviously sacrificing a lot for our sister. You should be proud of yourself."

Brit fought with the urge to deck his brother, as he had so many times when they were boys. Instead, he contented himself with slapping him on the side of his head. "Shut up, will you?"

Ross grinned as he rubbed his head. "All right, tough guy. But when you get tired of dealing with all her complications, let me know. That's what family is for."

. . .

Brit rejoined Tori on the bench, wedging himself between her and a balding, middle-aged man who stood up and screamed at his son at regular intervals. Tori ignored him, moving her leg farther and farther away until she was sitting at an angle, her back almost completely to him. She seemed to be making a point of enjoying herself. With everyone but him. In fact, she seemed to have taken a sudden and complete dislike to the man who had brought her to this happy family gathering.

He told himself it was a positive development. She and Melissa were hitting it off and there was no chance she expected more from him than he was interested in giving. His plan was working. Yet for some reason, after an hour or so of the silent treatment, he was becoming annoyed. When

Tori and Melissa wandered away to get a drink from a water fountain and Tori shot him a look of downright loathing, his irritation peaked. What had he done to deserve her distaste?

When they returned around the side of the bleachers, Tori and Melissa looked at each other and giggled. In case he hadn't understood that they were laughing at him, Melissa shot a sideways glance at Brit, and the two of them erupted into peals of laughter.

Ross elbowed him and whispered, "I think your plan is working."

"I can see that," Brit said. He bared his teeth in an approximation of a smile and asked Joe about his latest project—a mixed-use housing development in New Jersey. As Joe began rambling about the challenges of securing funding for affordable units, his attention turned back to Tori. When she sat down on the other side of Melissa, as far away from him as possible, and sent one more withering look his direction, he'd had enough.

He excused himself to Joe, apologized to the Balding Screamer, and jumped out of the stands. "Tori, we've got that thing at four." He nodded at Joe. "Tell Luke I thought he did a great job today."

Delia rush out of the stands and caught him around the knee. "Don't go!"

Brit threw her up in the air and gave her a last tickle before handing her back to Ross. Matt and Julia started to protest until he said, "I'll see you two for dinner next week, remember? Grandma and Grandpa are coming to town."

All three kids appeared mollified by the thought of seeing Grandma and Grandpa. Probably because Grandma and Grandpa usually brought presents whenever they returned from one of their trips.

Ever since his parents had retired, they'd been living the life they'd always wanted. Brit's dad, John, spent time every day painting and drawing, while Brit's mom, Phoebe, read through most of the great Russian authors. They sold the old brick house in Queens where Brit had grown up and moved to a tiny condo in SoHo. They went to gallery openings of obscure artists. His father's uniform now consisted of a pair of paint-stained khaki pants and white T-shirts, while his mother wore flowing skirts, scarves, and caftans. They were happier than he'd ever seen them.

Not that he begrudged them the change. But it would have been a bit easier to swallow if part of their joy hadn't stemmed from their complete lack of parental duties. They seemed to revel in their lack of responsibility. When Brit told them about what had happened to Melissa, they made worried noises for approximately five minutes before his father asked if Brit had seen his latest effort in watercolor, and his mother wondered out loud if her new oil painting looked better by the kitchen, or in the bedroom.

When it came right down to it, neither of his parents were particularly...well...*parental*. As long as Brit could remember, John had been hesitant, nervous, and tense. He was by nature an absentminded man with no head for details, and no stomach for the loud and physical antics of three active boys. John had inherited Excorp from his father, and been strong-armed into running it when his father's health had failed. It was a role that never suited him. By the time he was thirteen, Brit had become the default leader of the family, forced into that role by his father's refusal to take it.

Yes, John and Phoebe were much happier now. They relished the role of grandparent, where they could swoop down and deliver presents, receive adoration from their grandchildren, and then leave before they were asked to assume any responsibility.

Delia squeezed Brit's hand. "I wuv Grandma," she said. "But I like you better."

He mussed her hair and gave her another hug. "I love you too, pumpkin."

Tori was standing next to them, her body stiff with some unnamed frustration. Still, she managed to give Delia a friendly grin and say good-bye to Melissa and the others with an easy, genuine manner that was belied by the tense set of her shoulders.

As they began walking back to the car, Brit tamped down his own frustration. He couldn't afford to alienate her completely, not now, when he was so close to success. He tried for calm. Perhaps she hadn't liked being left on her own with Melissa. Perhaps she had felt ignored. Women didn't like feeling ignored.

He used his most soothing, appreciative tone. "Thanks for coming with me. They're nice kids, aren't they? They seemed to take to you right away."

She did not look at him, but her sandals slapped against the sidewalk as her pace increased.

He cleared his throat. Things were worse than he had thought. It was like walking next to a time bomb. "Er, is there something I should know about?"

"I'm not discussing it right now." She bit out each word with a tight, military precision. "If I discussed it right now, I'd have to kill you with my bare hands. I'd prefer to wait until we get back to your apartment, so I can use a knife, or a blunt instrument."

"I see." He nodded, his mind sorting through possible reasons for the fury that shook her narrow shoulders. "That makes sense."

"I might break a nail."

"Of course."

They walked in silence to the car, which was parked a few blocks from the park under the shade of a large linden tree. Brit opened Tori's door first, before walking around to the driver's side. He pulled open his door and left it open for a moment to let the heat disperse. Tori sat down on the hot leather seat, her face slowly turning from pink to red.

"Looks like you're ready to leave." Brit slid into the car and turned the air-conditioning on full blast. They drove the twenty-five minutes back to his place in silence.

The bomb continued to tick while Brit racked his brain for the reason why.

As they pulled to the curb beside his building, a terrible, sinking feeling settled over him. She had figured it out. Somehow, in the midst of all that bonding with Melissa, she had figured out his plan. It was the only explanation.

Brit jumped from the car and handed the keys to the valet. Tori stalked up to the front door, gave the doorman a polite nod, and marched inside. Following a few paces behind, Brit grimaced as Seth's eyes met his.

"Looks like you've got trouble, Mr. Bencher," Seth whispered.

"You don't know the half of it, Seth."

They rode the elevator a few steps apart. A soft chime announced the penthouse, and Brit motioned for Tori to precede him. "I'd appreciate it if you didn't slam the front door. The stained glass is fragile."

"I'll slam it if I damn well please," she growled.

"All right then." Though it was hardly a good time, his eyes lingered on her backside as she marched up the hall. Tori pissed off was even hotter than Tori not pissed off.

He unlocked the door for her and watched the swing of her hips as she walked through the entryway. Her hair was fast escaping the bonds of her ponytail, and it settled around her shoulders like a cloud of light following an avenging angel. He caught the door that she sent flying back at him, and then entered the apartment behind her.

Her voice lashed out like a whip. "You set me up."

"What do you mean?" He followed her into the kitchen,

putting himself in front of the block of knives.

Better safe than sorry.

"I knew there was a reason you wanted to go out with me." She threw her hands up in the air. "How could I be so stupid?"

He feigned confusion. "What are you talking about?"

"You, me, this whole thing!" She gestured wildly, and more of her halo escaped its confinement. "The suave, debonair Brit Bencher spending his time with a short, frizzy-haired attorney? It never made any sense. Except now it does. You wanted me to help your sister."

He swallowed hard. "What do you mean?"

She marched over and pointed at him, her eyes cold. "You slept with me because I know Garth Solen."

He sighed with relief. "Now that's absurd. I slept with you because I wanted you. I still want you." Here, at least, he could be absolutely honest.

"You're lying. You didn't invite me to that baseball game because you enjoy my company. You wanted me to meet your sister. You were hoping we'd hit it off. She told me that you sent her resume to Garth and he wouldn't meet with her. You wanted an invitation and you thought I could give it to you. Tell me that's not true."

He tried to speak, but the words lodged in his throat.

She leaped on his silence. "I knew it. Damn you, and damn me for falling for it." She turned around and stomped into the living room and picked up a cordless phone. "How do I get a cab?"

He half expected to see tears in her eyes, but they were clear and narrow, sparkling with hate. Hate for him, hate for herself, or perhaps some of both. He couldn't tell. Either way, it made him sick.

"Tori, slow down. Okay, I admit that I hoped you and Melissa would hit it off. But it's not like that was the only reason I—"

"A cab," she cut him off. "All I need is a cab."

"At least let me explain."

"What's to explain? You teased me with The Slayer's charm and good looks until I was a female idiot, and it was all a game to get what you wanted."

"Wait a minute." He started to channel some of his own anger, if only to replace the horrible, guilty feeling building in his gut. "You're the one who has been falling over backward to tell me we aren't dating. You *wanted* a one-night stand. As far as I can tell, you went out of your way to make sure I knew that I was nothing more than a warm body to you. So I slowed you down and forced you to meet my sister. I'm sorry. But it's not like I engaged in some kind of industrial espionage. I didn't steal your contact list or hack your computer."

Brit's chest rose and fell with the force of his words. Weeks of fear and worry coalesced in a rush. "Yes, I took you out to dinner because I wanted Solen's number. Can you blame me? Did you *see* Melissa?" His throat clenched. "She's my little sister, Tori. I'd do anything for her."

Tori threw down the phone. "I'm not a monster, Brit. If you had been honest with me, I might have been willing to help. But you weren't honest. You lied. You used me. You're exactly like every other charming, lying man, and I was stupid enough to fall for it."

"What are you talking about?" Brit sensed that Tori's look of pain went deeper than what he'd done.

"Forget it." She threw down the phone and grabbed her purse from the rack by the door. Extracting her BlackBerry, she turned her back on him and started down the hall toward the bedroom. "Yes, for Manhattan? I need the number for a taxi service. Any taxi service."

He snatched the device from her hand and ended the call. "Is this about your ex-fiancé? Is that why you're so upset? Did he cheat on you or something?"

"I'm not upset about Phil, and no, he didn't cheat on me." Tori spoke through lips tight with anger. "I'm upset because you're an asshole, and because I should have known better."

As he stared at her, he recalled what she had said at breakfast—something he had barely heard, so focused was he on Melissa and his plan.

"Your father, right? That's what this is about."

She gasped, and he could see the pain lance through her. Instantly, he regretted his words.

Smooth, Brit. That really helped. Can you find another emotional scar to rip open?

"Don't you dare try to psychoanalyze me," Tori hissed. "This weekend was obviously a huge mistake. Now give me my phone."

She leaned in to grab the phone. As she did her breasts bounced against his side and a painful jolt of electricity shot through him, from chest to groin. He caught her around the waist with one arm and pulled her closer, moving the phone over his head. Pushing against his chest with both hands, she squirmed to try to break his hold.

"Tori, I screwed up. I'm sorry. But I wasn't lying about this."

He leaned into her and she froze, staring at him with eyes as wide and panicked as a doe. Unable to stop himself, he traced the line of her jaw, and then touched her mouth with his own. She did not push away.

He pushed against the seam of her lips with his tongue until she opened her mouth and let him explore. His erection hardened. God he wanted her. He dropped the phone to the ground and wrapped both arms around her waist, then lifted her up so the length of her body rubbed against him. He traced the outline of her buttocks, the full curves begging to be cupped. Gently, he butted against her with his hips, until he felt her legs relax and part.

Still holding her against him, he spun around slowly and pushed her against the wall. Rapidly losing control, he lowered his hands to her thighs, pulling them up until she straddled him. Her muscles tightened beneath his fingers, until they surrounded him, gripped him. The moment his groin met the warm, welcoming spot between her legs, he groaned and thrust hard against her.

"I want you," he said, barely resisting the urge to rip off her pants. "Can't you see that? Yes, I admit I asked you out because of Solen, but this weekend was more than that. You've got to believe me."

She dropped her head against his shoulder. Somehow his words had hit her like a bucket of cold water. Her legs dropped to the floor and her hands pushed against his chest.

Slowly, she raised her head. Their eyes locked.

"No more, Brit," she said. "I can't handle more lies." Her anger had changed in a heartbeat to something dark. Something sad.

A jolt of pain shot through him.

He had put that look in her eyes. He had hurt her.

"This is not a lie," he ground out. "I don't know what it is, but it's the furthest thing from a lie."

When he covered her mouth again, she whimpered and gave a tiny, helpless push. "I can't do this. Please. Don't make me do this."

It was the whimper, like that of a hurt animal, that finally cut through his lust. He loosened his grip and she immediately twisted free and grabbed her BlackBerry from the ground. She flicked it on and studied it for a moment before clicking it into the holster at her waist. When she looked up at him, her eyes were bleak. She opened her mouth as if to speak, then shut it again and turned away.

He realized at that moment how tiny she really was. Her

spirit was so big—so feisty, moody, sexy—that he forgot she barely came to his shoulder. From behind, her shoulders looked delicate. Fragile.

Brit, you bastard, what have you done?

"Seth will get you a cab," he said.

She nodded and pushed past him to the hall.

He dropped his head and clenched and unclenched his fists. Fury and guilt mixed in equal measures in his gut.

You manipulated her. You knew exactly what you were doing.

He'd been lying to himself all along in an effort to assuage his guilt. He'd felt Tori's desire and used it against her. And now he realized that his betrayal went to the very heart of who she was.

He watched her gather her belongings, her back rigid with pride.

The enormity of what he'd done staggered him. He'd been so sure he could fix Melissa, the same way he'd fixed Excorp, that he'd been willing to sacrifice anyone—including Tori—who got in his way.

"There's no reason for you to keep playing stand-in father."

Ross's words rang in his ears. He'd been trying to fix them for years. All of them. And Tori had paid the price.

"I'm sorry," he said.

Without looking at him, Tori opened the front door and headed for the elevator. He watched her go with a feeling that had let something precious slip through his fingers, and he had no idea how to get it back.

• • •

As the cab pulled away from the curb, Tori started scrolling through e-mail messages, trying to ignore her shaking hands. The words trailed across the tiny screen, but none of them reached her brain.

She took a deep, shuddering breath and pushed her hair back from her face. What an idiot. She knew there was something going on the very first time he invited her to dinner. She knew she couldn't trust him. One look at that absurdly beautiful body and take-your-breath-away smile and she had known the truth. Brit was a walking lie.

Sure, he could get it up for her. But what did that prove? A man could get it up for a sheep.

Hot waves of shame forced her eyes closed. It would be a long time before she could forget her own willingness to be persuaded. When he kissed her, even after she knew the truth, she had been ready to melt into his arms. For the first time, Tori understood her mother's insistence that she stay away from charming men. Nothing could be worse than this feeling of helplessness in the face of a man's duplicity.

The truth was, if she hadn't figured out about Melissa, she would have been in serious danger of falling for him. For all her brave words about keeping the weekend light and emotion-free, in two short days he had swept past her carefully constructed barriers and left her vulnerable to the sort of pain she'd been working all her life to avoid.

Images of his strong hands, the way he touched her back when they walked, and the dark light of passion in his eyes flashed before her like scenes from a movie. A shiver passed down her spine and she opened her eyes immediately.

Ruthlessly, she quashed the hurt, the shame and helplessness, and focused instead on Brit's accusation that she had treated him as nothing more than a warm body.

That's right, you bastard, she thought fiercely. *This meant nothing to me. Nothing at all.*

So she had gotten what she wanted, and learned a lesson at the same time. A lesson she wouldn't forget for a long, long time.

Chapter Fourteen

"Betsy, have you heard from Karl yet?" Tori stuck her head into the hallway and called to her assistant, who was pulling a stack of papers from the printer.

"Yeah, he arrived an hour ago and I forgot to tell you," Betsy sniped, as she trotted the rest of the way back to her desk and started sorting through the papers. She handed two documents to Tori and set down the rest in a stack by her desk. "Here's your Monday morning treat—the report from the diligence team. They've got two employee complaints we need to investigate, a couple of litigation matters, and there's some problems with the stock options."

"What?" Tori grabbed the papers and frowned. "Damn it, I thought our folks had already looked at that."

"I guess they looked again. Oh, and Brit called."

Tori tightened her mouth and did not look up. "I told you I'm not interested in talking to him."

"You're taking the whole 'he lied to me' thing a bit far, aren't you?" Betsy asked. "He obviously feels terrible about it. Why not punish him in person? Let him do his penance. I can think of lots of ways for a man like that to do penance."

Tori shook her head. "I don't need more people in my life whom I can't trust."

"You only care because you were falling for him," Betsy threw out as Tori turned around and headed back into her office.

"I'm not talking about this."

"You can't keep running away from life, Tori." Betsy followed a few paces behind.

"Who are you, Dr. Phil?" Tori slammed into her chair and threw the papers on the desk in front of her.

"You don't need Dr. Phil to know that there's something weird going on when an intelligent, beautiful woman like you buries herself in her work, dates guys with the personality of a wet noodle, and refuses to talk to the first decent guy she's slept with in years, even after he calls five times in two weeks."

Tori tried to screw her face into something intimidating. "Four times, and we aren't discussing it. Now about these employee complaints—"

"He said he's going to stop calling. He's getting ready for a trip. To Scotland."

Tori tried not to visibly react. Brit was going to Scotland? Was he finally taking the trip he'd always dreamed about? "Why don't you date him?" she said. "You're obviously very close."

Betsy pressed a dramatic hand against her forehead. "For The Slayer, I'd leave Jimmy and the kids and head to Scotland before you could say, 'A canna sell the cou an sup the milk.'"

Tori snorted, unable to restrain a smile. "What in the world does that mean?"

"I'm not sure, but I think it was Scottish for 'you can't have it all.'"

"You've been memorizing Scottish phrases?"

"I thought Brit would appreciate it."

"You," Tori drawled, "are pathetic."

"I do it all for you," Betsy replied. "We've gotten quite close, you know. He may be The Slayer, but I think he's actually a very sweet man."

"Brit is not sweet. He's a rat. A miserable, lying rat."

"He messed up and he's sorry, Tori. Can't you give him a break?"

Tori pictured herself punching Brit right in the middle of his crooked nose. "I'd love to give him a break. Just not the kind you're suggesting."

"I think he wants you to go to Scotland with him. He mentioned the trip to me in passing, but he obviously wants you to know about it."

"Brit and I are done. If he's calling, it's because he's a bigger liar than I thought, or he's got a guilty conscience. Either way, I want nothing to do with him."

"That is the biggest load of bull I have ever heard," Betsy pronounced. "And I work at a law firm. I've heard a lot of bull."

Tori tucked a relatively calm, controlled ringlet behind one ear. She'd been trying a new hair product lately: it combined horsetail and some tree nut grown only on a remote mountain in Brazil. The stuff cost its weight in gold, but it kept Tori's curls from frizzing, so she paid the price gratefully.

She had to hand that to Brit. Even though he had practically ripped out her heart and stomped on it with his beautiful Italian loafers, he had given her something. She didn't know how to describe it, but she felt earthier, more sensual since she'd been with him. Like her body was still blooming, even two weeks later, from the warmth of his sexual attention. Days after she returned from New York she began finding herself in the beauty aisle of her local market, studying lotions, hair gels, and makeup with more attention than she'd given them for years.

"Can we not talk about this right now? I have work to do." Tori picked up the papers and shook them in front of Betsy's face.

Betsy nodded. "I know. You're scared. You've finally found a man who might be worthy of you. By all means, don't think about it."

"Betsy, I've got a mountain of work like you've never seen. Karl Bulcher is breathing down my neck like a rabid dog, I have a confidentiality leak, disclosure issues, and these employee complaints are driving me nuts. Do you really think this is a good time to discuss my personal life? Can't you see I have no time for a personal life?"

"You have to make time," Betsy said.

"Let it go," Tori ground out. "I'm really not in the mood."

Something in Tori's voice must have finally penetrated Betsy's extra-dense skull, because she stood and headed for the door, adjusting her carefully hairsprayed locks with one red-lacquered fingernail. "Fine. I'll tell him you're not interested. But when you're sixty and would give everything in your power to get him back, don't come crying to me."

At that moment, the phone on Tori's desk rang, startling them both. She looked at the number—a 212 area code. "I'm not answering it, Betsy."

Betsy ran to her phone as fast as her giant platform heels would allow and grabbed her phone from the opposite side of the desk. "Tori Anderson's office." There was a pause, then she said, "I'll see if she's available."

Betsy poked her head back through the door. "It's Melissa Bencher. She's the sister, right? This is shaping up to be a fun morning. Want to take it?"

Tori drummed her fingers on the desk and stared at the

phone. Melissa? Why was Melissa calling?

"Okay," she said reluctantly.

"She's on line one," Betsy said.

Tori took a deep breath and picked up the phone. "Hi Melissa, what can I do for you?"

"Tori?" Melissa's soft voice, painfully reminiscent of her brother, echoed through the phone. "Listen, before you hang up, which I could fully understand if you wanted to do, let me say that I had nothing to do with whatever happened at the park. Brit's sort of a caveman sometimes, and I'm really sorry if you got caught up in one of his Big Brother schemes."

Tori gritted her teeth. "Thanks. Now I'm really busy, so if you don't mind—"

"But that's not why I called."

"Okay—"

Melissa took a deep breath and made an obvious attempt to add strength to her voice. "I've got no right to ask this, and you'll probably say no, but I'm determined to give it a try."

Tori wound the phone cord around her finger. "Go ahead."

"Solen Labs is working on the same kind of technology that The Asshole and I were developing in our lab." Melissa's voice got higher and tenser. "But Solen's going about it all wrong. I know, because we failed. Spectacularly."

"You want me to call Garth and tell him to give up on his work? Sorry, Melissa, but—"

"No, no," Melissa interrupted. "It's complicated, but I developed a work-around to the problem. I was about to tell The Asshole when I found him screwing around on my kitchen table. The information is mine, and I want to share it with Solen. I want to work with him, Tori, and this is my way in."

"Did you tell Garth about this when you applied for a job?"

"That's the problem. I didn't apply for anything. I've wanted to work for Solen for years, even before I met The Asshole. My idiot brother knew that and sent in a resume, having no idea what the hell he was doing. Of course they rejected it."

"Why didn't you send in your own letter?"

"I haven't exactly been interested in a job, Tori. I needed to wallow for a little while. I might have been a little depressed."

Might have been?

Tori squashed the thought.

"I thought I'd never get through to Solen," Melissa continued. "But then I met you, and I realized I was giving up too soon." She paused, and Tori could hear her take a deep breath. "You're the only one who can get through to him, Tori. Can you help me?"

Tori released her finger and hit the *mute* button on the phone. Then she slammed her head repeatedly on the desk. There was only one logical answer to that question: no. If she had half a brain, she'd stay as far away from Brit and his troubled family as possible.

But Melissa was more than Brit's sister. She was a real, human person who needed help. Not to mention that she might be able to do something for Garth.

Tori was a sucker for needy, brilliant people. Especially ones who could make her clients a lot of money.

She pushed back her hair and unmuted the phone. "I'll want to make sure it's all legal first. You'll have to give me any documents you signed, plus I'll have to review some law before I'll talk to Garth. And I have one condition."

"What's that?"

"I never have to talk to your brother again."

• • •

A blast of early summer heat hit Tori the moment she opened her car door. She fought the urge to close the door and drive back to her office. Lately, she felt like this every time she pulled up to Langston Estates. A heavy weight would settle over her shoulders and a mix of sadness and dread would leave her sick and trembling.

Still, dread was a small price to pay for the guilt she otherwise carried around like Jacob Marley's chains if she didn't make it here for a visit.

Tori marched up the concrete path and smiled at a stranger who opened the door for her. The lobby was filled with guests and residents, the usual lunchtime rush. She waved to Harley, Chad's daytime counterpart at the front desk, and continued to her mother's room. Knocking gently, she took a deep breath, squared her shoulders, and pushed open the door.

The smell of Jeanne's cloying, musky perfume surrounded Tori like a blanket. Her mother sat up in the adjustable bed, staring sightlessly at the shrubbery outside her window. Jeanne plucked aimlessly at her comforter, almost but not quite in time with the rhythm of a Chopin waltz emanating from a small CD player by the back wall.

She gave her standard greeting as she approached. "Hi, Mom, it's me, Tori."

Jeanne moved her head and focused briefly on Tori's face before turning back to the window.

The knot in Tori's stomach eased. Her mother looked peaceful today, her face smooth, eyes calm. During the last few visits she had been tense and angry, wound so tightly it was inevitable that she would explode before Tori left.

"It's so nice and cool in here." Tori sat in the rocking chair beside the bed. "You wouldn't believe how hot it is outside. I guess all that business about global warming must be true, huh?"

Not expecting a response, Tori launched into a description of her day, of the work she was doing and her efforts to keep Karl happy. It felt good, to let the words spill out. Sometimes when she visited her mother she spent an entire hour talking, filling the silence with absurd anecdotes and stories about her job even though she knew her mother would never remember any of it.

"I won't be here on Friday. I'm taking the train to New York to meet with Melissa Bencher." Tori pushed herself to standing and walked from one end of the room to the other, rubbing her arms as she did. She tried to picture Melissa's face and cursed herself when Brit appeared instead. "It's probably a horrible idea," she admitted. "I know exactly what you'd say. I should never have taken her call. I should have hung up when I got the chance."

Jeanne's eyes followed Tori as she paced the length of the room, but it was impossible to know how much, if any, of the conversation she was following.

Tori brushed her hair back from her forehead. She stopped by the mirror on the rear wall of the room and examined her face. Were those new wrinkles around her mouth? She stuck out her tongue and turned another lap, her mother's voice ringing in her ears.

"Yes, I can hear you now," Tori said. "You'd tell me I'm crazy and asking for trouble. And I know you're right. I let Brit make a fool of me once, and if I'm not careful it could happen again.

"But I had to help Melissa. You understand that, don't you? It's not her fault her brother's a jerk. I won't make the mistake of trusting him again. Besides, Betsy told me that he's leaving the country soon. So I won't even have to see him."

Jeanne nodded solemnly. Tori slid back into the chair and leaned her shoulder and head against the mattress. She thought about the time she was in sixth grade, when a boy she liked had humiliated her in front of his friends. When she told her mother what had happened Jeanne hugged her fiercely, tightly, stroked her hair, and told her everything would be all right. Tori had never felt so protected before, or after.

"Mom? I wish I..." Her throat squeezed closed. She cleared it and started again, "I wish I knew what to do. I wish I knew how not to be so damn lonely. I miss you, you know. I miss you a lot."

She put her hand on the bedspread, close enough that she could feel the heat from her mother's body. Jeanne didn't always want to be touched, especially not lately, so Tori didn't try to take her hand. But then she felt her mother's head lean against hers, and Jeanne's gnarled, wrinkled hand moved a few inches closer on the bedspread.

"Thanks, Mom," Tori whispered.

They sat like that, barely touching, for a long time.

Chapter Fifteen

Four days later, Tori walked into Melissa's apartment on the Upper East Side and reminded herself one last time that she was only here for Melissa. The apartment was surely large by New York standards, but tiny compared with Tori's own comfortable bungalow back in Philadelphia; a single large room served as kitchen and living room, with a screen setting off the desk and work area. The blinking green lights of various devices shone through the bamboo, and Tori thought she saw the outlines of three computer monitors atop an L-shaped desk.

Like its owner, the setting was simple and efficient. Also like its owner, however, it had beauty in unexpected places, as Tori noticed when she slid her hand over the curve of an armrest, or sunlight would sparkle off the chrome leg of a chair. Even the building was disguised elegance—an old townhouse with steep steps and a crumbling walkway giving way to a glass-tiled entry with a row of antique mailboxes.

Melissa ushered Tori through a heavy wooden door and motioned for her to sit down in the small common area. Tori was relieved to see that she looked better than she had in the park. Melissa's long hair had been styled in soft waves around her face, and a light coat of mascara emphasized the glittering blue of her eyes. She brought out a china teapot with a pink and blue pattern shot with accents of gold, and offered Tori a cup.

"Thanks for coming. I know this all seems kind of crazy." Her voice was high and tight, and Tori had to lean forward to make out the words.

She was nervous.

"Not at all," Tori said.

It had actually been an enormous problem, necessitating three nights with very little sleep to get enough of her other work done so she could take the Thursday afternoon train to New York. She had reviewed Melissa's information on the way up and had been relieved to find that Melissa was right—no law would stop her from sharing her knowledge with Solen.

Melissa leaned forward to pour the tea. Her movements were quick, her hands visibly shaking. She tucked them in her lap and took a deep breath before looking up at Tori. "So… what do you think?"

"About Solen? Well, I gave Garth a call and he said he'd meet with you."

Melissa's breath spilled out in a rush.

"But he wants me there," Tori cautioned. "Not that I know the robotics business, but he's got some questions about the reason you want to work for him so badly, and I think we should probably decide how much of your story you want to tell."

"I see." Melissa carefully added a lump of lump of sugar to Tori's tea. "You're right, of course. I hadn't thought about that. I hope you know how much I appreciate this. If it hadn't been for meeting you the other day…well, I never would have even thought about doing something like this."

Tori decided not to tell her that she preferred her tea black. "Honestly, I probably wouldn't have gotten involved, but it sounds like in the long run, you'll be doing Garth a favor. The last thing I want is for him to try something at the lab that you know is a waste of time."

"I don't know for sure that I can do it." Melissa handed the cup to Tori, the delicate china rattling in the saucer. Staring down at the tea, she said, "Mark and I always worked together, before. This will be my first time on my own."

Tori leaned forward, taking the tea and setting it down on a sturdy cherry end table, then patted Melissa's hand. "You won't be alone. Garth will be there, too. You've never met a guy like him before. He's utterly brilliant, but completely without an ego. And I'll be around, too. You can call me if you need anything."

Melissa smiled for the first time. "I don't deserve your help."

"That's what women do," Tori said. "We help each other. Especially when it comes to moving on after lousy ex-boyfriends. But I'm not sure you really need my help anyway." She indicated a picture of Brit and Melissa on the edge of a bookshelf. "You've got more powerful friends in your court than me."

Melissa leaned back in the couch and rubbed her eyes. When she opened them, tears had pooled in the corners. She brushed them aside and took a deep breath before she said, "You have no idea how hard it is to be the most inadequate member of the Bencher family. I've had three brothers hovering over me as long as I can remember, all of them more confident, more put together, and more successful than I am. Brit's the worst. He's only seven years older than I am, but you'd think it was twenty."

"Is that right?" Tori cleared her throat. The last thing in

the world she wanted to do was talk about Brit. "Well, we should go over some of the specifics for tomorrow. We're meeting at the hotel—"

"He got it in his head at some point that our parents weren't very good at their jobs," Melissa continued, "so he decided to take up the slack. I can't tell you how frustrating it is. The moment I got to New York, he started hovering over me like I was a broken doll. I kept telling him I needed some space, but he never listened. And then he got you involved. Well, I felt horrible about that. But I suppose I can't blame him completely. It did give me the idea for doing this."

"Okay, so about tomorrow—"

"He's really very gentle, you know, under all that bossy-CEO crap," Melissa sailed on, as if Tori had not spoken. "And he loves kids. You saw him with Delia. He'll make an excellent father someday. I have no idea why he's so scared of dating someone with a brain."

It seemed rather obvious to Tori, but she figured it would be better not to point that out. "The conference room is on the second floor of the hotel. It's not pretty, but I thought it would be best to find a neutral setting."

Melissa nodded. "Great. Brit's been grumpier than a bear these past two weeks, you know. Snaps my head off if I even mention your name. I've never seen him that way about a woman. I thought he was going to blow a gasket the other night at dinner when Ross teased him about you. That was when I knew something interesting was going on. I know you said you weren't dating, but, er, I don't suppose…I mean, is there any chance?"

There it was. The question Tori had suspected was coming.

"No," she said flatly.

"Hmm. You're sure about that, are you? Because I know it seems like he went out with you because of me, but it looks to me like there's a lot more going on."

"I'm sure. Now, can we please talk about the reason I'm here? We only have tonight, and I want to make sure we get our story straight."

Melissa sighed, but did not mention Brit again.

• • •

It was well past ten o'clock before Tori stood up and rubbed her eyes. Once she got Melissa past her nerves they struck up a comfortable rapport, and their conversation had quickly gone far beyond preparing for a job interview.

Tori's schedule didn't leave her much time for friends, and she realized it had been months—years?—since she'd had an evening with another woman to sit around and talk. They'd had dinner, and managed to put away two bottles of wine. Melissa told her all about her ex-boyfriend Mark, and Tori found herself confiding things about her mother that she'd never told another soul.

Finally, she couldn't deny her body's demand for sleep. "Look, I hate to say it but I'm tipsy and my eyes are starting to close. I need to get some rest before tomorrow or I'll embarrass both of us."

Melissa flushed. "I'm sorry. I get to talking about things and it's hard to stop. I'll call you a cab right away."

"Don't apologize." Tori grinned, feeling a pleasant buzz in her head. "It was the best night I've had in a long time."

A buzzer sounded. Tori jumped at the unexpected noise.

Melissa crossed to a white intercom by the door and pushed a button. "Hello?"

"Melissa, let me up."

The rush of adrenaline began the moment Tori heard the voice. Deep, rich, he might as well have been saying, "Lean back. Let me take care of you," as he had in Sam Huo's office.

"Brit, what are you doing here? I'm on my way out," Melissa said.

"Where are you going? I'll give you a ride."

Melissa let go of the button and gave Tori a questioning look.

Tori shook her head. "Please," she said, hating the desperation in her voice. "It would be easier if we didn't have to talk."

"Why don't we have dinner tomorrow?" Melissa said into the white box.

"Because Ross told me you have something going on tomorrow morning that you didn't want to tell me about, and I've been worried sick that you called that bastard ex-boyfriend of yours. I've been calling for the past two hours but you refuse to pick up your cell. Either you let me up now or I'm waiting here until you come down."

Melissa released the button and winced at Tori. "I'm sorry. I told Ross you were coming into town. He really took a liking to you. But I told him not to tell Brit what was going on." She leaned back on the button. "Look, Brit, I didn't call Mark, okay? You can go home now."

"Melissa. I need to talk to you. Let me up." Brit's voice took on that deadly quiet tone that was inexplicably terrifying.

Tori screwed together what was left of her courage. There was no reason to leave Melissa to fight her battles. She motioned Melissa aside and pushed the intercom. "Brit, it's Tori. Melissa and I are meeting with Solen tomorrow. Are you happy?"

There was a long pause. Then, "Tori?"

"Yes, Tori," Melissa barked into the wall, throwing back her head defiantly as if he were right beside her. "So you can see I'll be fine."

"Tori's there now?"

Melissa turned to Tori and threw her hands up in the air.

"He isn't usually this dense."

With a feeling of certain doom, Tori grabbed her purse and small suitcase and gave Melissa an artificial smile. "We might as well face him now, right? No sense putting it off."

Though they had only known each other for a short time, Melissa's quick squeeze of Tori's arm felt like that of an old friend. "He's like a middle school boy," Melissa said. "He's meanest to the girls he really likes."

"Why doesn't that make me feel better?" Tori asked.

They headed down the stairs, Tori's heart beating faster with every step. Her fingers began to tingle and her face got hot, even though the air in the unheated stairway was cool. The last time she had seen Brit, he had come close to stealing every bit of pride and self-respect she had. But tonight would be different. She would be cool and composed. She would not let him rattle that composure.

She would not.

You were nothing more than a warm body, Brit Bencher...

They passed the mailboxes. On the stoop outside, Tori could see Brit glowering at the front door. He looked menacing in the single yellow light, his face a series of moving shadows.

"I'll go first," Melissa said.

Grateful for her presence, Tori willingly dropped back.

Melissa opened the door and held it behind her for Tori. "Why don't you save the scene for the next Big Brothers Anonymous," she said, when all three of them were crowded together on the small, cracked concrete front step.

He did not remove his hands from the pockets of his dark pants. He must have come from work because he still wore a dark blue suit, though he lacked a tie and the top button of his crisp white shirt was undone. Her breath caught at the sight of him, harder and more masculine than she could have imagined.

Nothing but a warm body...

With a curl of his lips that drew Tori's gaze to that obscenely sensual mouth, he ignored Melissa completely. "You came back," he said, focusing his icy-hot stare on Tori.

"I'm not here for you," she said, hoping he wouldn't hear the quiver in her voice. "I'm here for Melissa."

Brit turned to his sister. "You can go back up. I'll take Tori home."

Melissa looked between them. "She's tired. I was about to call her a cab."

"Tori and I need to talk," he said.

"I'm not leaving." Melissa assumed a stubborn stance, legs spread several feet apart, arms akimbo.

"Don't be ridiculous." His voice took on that smooth, persuasive tone that Tori remembered so well. "I've got my driver here. We can drop Tori off at her hotel. There's no reason to pay for a cab."

Tori wanted to scream no, but pride kept her voice at a reasonable volume. "I would prefer the taxi."

"Now that's just plain silly," Brit said. "Unless you're too nervous to ride in the same car with me."

"You're a bully, you know that?" Melissa said.

"Give up, sis," Brit said. "I know you don't want me camping out on your stoop." He relaxed against the iron railing on the side of the steps, his posture one of supreme confidence.

Tori hitched her purse higher on her shoulder and surrendered to the inevitable. With an attempt at a comforting smile, she patted Melissa lightly on the shoulder. "This is ridiculous. There's no reason for the two of you to fight over a simple cab ride. It won't kill me to go to the hotel with him. You need to get some sleep."

"If you're sure," Melissa said, glaring at Brit.

"I'm sure. I'll see you tomorrow at eight."

After a worried sigh, Melissa gave Tori a quick hug, glared at her brother, and went back inside. Tori squared her shoulders and thought about her one-way conversation with her mother a few days before.

You said you'd learned your lesson. Now prove it.

He motioned toward her suitcase. "Why don't you let me take your bag?"

"No." She clutched it tightly against her.

The black Mercedes purred on the street in front of them. Brit walked between two parked cars and opened the door. "Fine. After you."

Careful not to brush against him, she ducked inside and jerked her suitcase across the smooth leather seat, propping it up like a barrier between them.

Brit pulled the door closed behind him. "Where are we headed?" he asked Tori.

"The Grand Hyatt."

"You aren't very adventurous."

"I'm too adventurous," she corrected. "I won't make that mistake again."

He leaned forward and said something to the driver, then laid her suitcase flat on the seat and studied her. "You won't take my calls."

"I told you I wanted nothing more to do with you." In the dark interior of the car, his presence seemed larger than life, and more threatening.

"I said I was sorry. What more can I do?"

"How about leave me alone? I know it's hard to believe, but some women really aren't interested in your attention. I happen to be one of them."

He reached one hand across her suitcase and let it brush against her arm. "So you aren't interested in this?"

The empty space between them shrank, and tendrils of nervous anticipation slithered from Tori's belly to her knees.

"Exactly," she said.

"What about this?" He took her unprotesting hand and traced a lazy pattern on the soft skin between her thumb and forefinger.

"Definitely not." She wished she could pull her hand from his grasp but found herself helpless under the rhythmic stroking.

"You are the most contrary woman I've ever met."

"You are a liar and a cheat," she whispered. She tried to muster images of her mother, but Brit's gentle, rhythmic stroking inhabited every corner of her brain. They rode in silence for a long time, the heat slowly rising until every muscle in Tori's body strained for the next touch, for deeper, more significant contact.

"I'm going to Scotland," he said suddenly.

"Betsy told me."

"I leave in a month."

The finality in Brit's tone penetrated the haze of pleasure his touch had created. "What about Excorp?"

"I'm taking an indefinite leave from Excorp." He released her hand to run his fingers through his hair. "I told the board today."

Tori sat upright. "Really? I suppose I should have guessed, from the way you were talking the other day. But why?"

"Because of you." He angled his body so he could look directly into her eyes. "I realized after you left that I'd been acting like an ass. I should never have tried to fool you and Melissa that way. I've been trying to micromanage Melissa's life. And a lot of other lives, too." His eyes swallowed her face and licked hungrily at the neckline of her snug T-shirt.

She tried to look away, but he had her trapped. "What does that have to do with Excorp?"

"I took over Excorp like I took over running my family.

But as Melissa tells me several times a day, she's all grown up, and Excorp is, too. I've never taken a vacation, Tori. Never. But I should. That's why I kept calling. I wanted to tell you I realized how stupid I'd been. I started making plans to take some time off the day you left."

"Oh." Tori leaned back in the seat, trying to digest what he was saying. He had called her to apologize for being an idiot, not because he wanted to see her again. And now he was leaving for Scotland. "How long will you be gone?"

He laughed and rubbed his face as he slouched back in the seat. "I have no idea. I can't tell you how wonderful that feels. Maybe a month. Maybe a two. I'm going to travel, develop a fake accent, and maybe grow a beard."

"Fantastic," Tori said. She swallowed hard and mustered a fake smile. "I can't believe you're really going to do it. Talk about reclaiming your lost youth."

He chuckled and opened his eyes. "I know, it's crazy. But enough about me. How did you end up at Melissa's place? When I heard from Ross that she had some meeting set up tomorrow, I thought I was going to blow a gasket. I realize I said I was going to treat her like an adult, but I was terrified she was going to go back to that bastard Mark."

"She called me a few days ago." Tori explained Melissa's plan to help Solen Labs with their latest initiative. "I can't guarantee that he'll hire her, but I think it's great that she's trying. At least it will help her get out of the house."

Brit's smile threatened to split his face. It transformed all the hard lines of his jaw and cheekbones. "That's great. I can't tell you how happy that makes me. Though I do have one concern." His voice took on a serious tone, and he sat straighter in the seat.

"What?"

"Now that there's no question of ulterior motives, does that mean I get to see you again?"

Dangerous territory.

Like pulling petals off of a daisy.

He loves me, he loves me not…

"I told you I wasn't going to do this again, Brit."

His gaze turned coaxing. "That's because you were hurt. I understand that. But things are different now. You understand that I'm a man, and I'm destined to do stupid things. The Melissa fiasco was one of those things." His smile faded, and a serious, hungry look took its place, leaving her trembling. "Thanks to my desire to fix everyone's life but my own, you got the impression that I didn't really want you. Which is nonsense. Truth is, I can't think of anything I want more."

The car pulled to a slow stop. Tori looked out, but did not see the lights of the Hyatt. Instead, she saw the gleam of an antique streetlight.

Tori shook her head, though what she saw wasn't really much of a surprise. "This isn't my hotel."

Chapter Sixteen

He had the grace to look embarrassed. "You're right. It's my place. I was hoping…"

She fought the answering smile that tickled the corners of her mouth.

He loves me…

"You don't take no for an answer, do you?"

"You promised me a weekend, and I got a day. You owe me one more night."

"I don't owe you anything."

Brit jumped out of the car and offered his hand. "We had a deal. As an attorney, you have to respect that."

"I never signed anything."

"It was a verbal agreement. Fully enforceable."

"Lord, save me from the CEO trying to play lawyer." She groaned, but found her hand slipping into his.

She was being stupid. Irresponsible. She had vowed to stay away from him.

He's nothing more than a warm body, Mom. I won't fall for him. I swear it.

Brit waved good-bye to his driver and tugged her through the front door. They barely made it into the elevator before he looped one possessive arm around her waist and slid the other around her jaw.

His thumb traced a path over her lips, and she closed her eyes.

"Damn it, Brit."

Cool lips followed his thumb.

She tensed, but did not push away. He deepened the kiss, claiming her with the confidence of a man who anticipates no resistance. Anger shot through her with unexpected heat. He was always in control. For once, she wanted to be the one driving this train.

Lightly, she bit his lip and then lapped it with her tongue, teased him with darting, feathery kisses until he growled in frustration and ground his mouth against hers. Something powerful took over her body, leaving her prisoner to an unfamiliar mixture of lust and fury. Dragging his face lower, she buried her tongue in his mouth, drinking deeply from him and then pulling away when he attempted to reciprocate.

"You're going to punish me, aren't you?" he whispered, breathing heavily.

"Do you deserve to be punished?"

"Hell yes." He slipped his hands lower to cup her buttocks and ease her against his lean hips. "Let me make it up to you. I screwed up—I did—but I can't fake this. Surely you know that."

Still caught in the grip of an unholy passion, she locked eyes with him, ground her pelvis against his hardness, then deliberately jerked away. When the elevator doors opened, she walked out first, emphasizing the swing of her hips.

He followed a step behind her, reaching up to cup her breasts. When his thumbs trailed across her nipples, she stopped and let him touch her, then drew her hands up to break the contact.

"Not yet," she hissed. "You'll have to wait."

He opened the door to his apartment and stumbled inside. She closed the door behind them and grabbed the lapels of his jacket, tugging it down over his shoulders. The soft wool slipped to the ground with a soft rustle. He started toward her, but she held up one hand.

"No," she said.

Trembling, she slipped off her own jacket and pulled the thin T-shirt over her head. Her breasts ached for contact, so she slid her hands over the taut skin, teasing the already firm peaks. Needing more, she rolled the nipples between her thumb and forefinger, closing her eyes for a moment to revel in the pleasure-pain she was inflicting.

Brit stepped forward, his eyes glassy. "You are incredible," he said, his voice hoarse. "Please. Let me touch you."

She grabbed him by the shirt and tugged his face down to hers, allowing him only a brief kiss before pushing him away. "Follow me."

She made her way to the bedroom, kicking off her shoes and then unhooking her bra as she went. When she reached Brit's room, she turned to find him unbuttoning his own shirt. "Good," she said, tracing the outline of her lips with the tip of her tongue. "Very good."

"Tori—"

"No!" The voice sounded like it came from a stranger. "You don't get to make the rules tonight. I do."

She unzipped her pants and let them fall to the floor. Then she climbed on the bed, propping herself on pillows so she could watch him standing in front of her.

Slowly, his gaze pinned to hers, Brit removed the rest of his clothes. Tori stroked her breasts as she watched, her body and mind given over to the surge of power and need that raced through her.

Finally, he approached the bed. Tori's eyes covered the length of his beautiful olive skin, the dark crinkling hair on his chest, and his powerful erection. "May I?" he asked hoarsely.

Tori nodded. Nothing would satisfy her now but him.

Laying her head back on the comforter, she closed her eyes and stretched her arms over her head. The bed dipped when he knelt beside her. She could feel the heat emanating from him, brushing her skin like a delicate caress. He slid the back of one hand against her side and she shivered.

With agonizing, steady movements, he caressed the delicate skin of her breast, circling the areola with his tongue before taking her nipple into his mouth. The gentle pressure of his lips sent her hips jerking forward.

"More," she commanded. "Harder."

Brit obliged, applying increasing pressure and heat, finally nipping at the tender flesh. When soft mewling sounds were coming from somewhere deep in her throat, he slid one hand across her rib cage and down to her mound.

"I've been imagining you like this for the past two weeks," he whispered. "I can't get you out of my mind."

His fingers tickled her stomach, tugged down the soft lace of her panties. Stealthy kisses followed everywhere his hands touched, on the rounded curve of her belly, along the side of her hip, in the soft flesh behind her knee. Keeping her body utterly still, Tori let the magic of his mouth wash away the hurt and the anger, leaving behind only a steady, glowing need. When his warm breath tickled her mound, she moaned and thrust against him.

He pushed gently on her knees. "Open for me, Tori. Let me love you."

Shameless with desire, she let her legs fall open and offered herself to him. Her heart skipped when he drew a short, harsh breath. Imagining her own lush, pink curves open to him, glistening with dew, she arched her hips and forced her muscles to relax.

He slid over her, breathing gently on her soft, wet flesh until she tangled her fingers in his hair and pressed him against her. He lapped the edges of her skin and let his tongue follow a path around the edges of her clit. When she was almost ready to scream, he looked up with a twinkle in his eyes.

"Shall I continue?"

"Yes," she said, her voice somewhere between a moan and a scream.

He drew himself across her body, stopping to roll her nipples between his fingers. She half expected to see steam rise between them when he moved his hips and the heat of his erection touched the damp warmth between her legs.

He butted against her. Each touch was like a shock that sent her hips moving to meet him. Her nipples swayed gently as she moved, and he covered one with his mouth, tugging gently at first, and then harder, until she sobbed and threaded her fingers through his hair.

"Yes," she breathed, "please, yes."

A trail of kisses took him from her breasts to the soft skin of her stomach. One hand traced a path back toward her breasts, to torment her hard, hurting nipples while his mouth moved lower. When his tongue returned to the needy flesh below she jerked against him, crying out with the pain and pleasure he was inflicting. His back flexed under her fingers, the muscles standing out in sharp relief under her nails, but she did not want to dissolve like this. She wanted him inside her, driving her into oblivion.

Almost mindless with desire, she pulled him up, hoping he would understand her silent plea. He buried his face in her navel, breathing hard as if striving for control.

"Don't make me wait," she said. "I want you now."

"And if I want to wait?" He leaned back on his haunches, a beautiful male animal surveying his mate.

"You won't," she said, dropping her hands down to caress his tight buttocks.

"Stop that," he growled, catching her hands and leaving a kiss on each palm. "I need to concentrate for a second."

He rifled through a bedside table and withdrew a foil-wrapped packet. Tori grabbed the condom and unrolled it herself, sliding it over his length with a shaking hand. She caressed him, closing her fingers around the base of him and riding his length.

"No more games," she said. "I need you now."

With a groan he fell forward, and her hand came between them to guide him into her. When he was buried deep inside, he stopped. Tori wanted to sob with the pleasure of the moment. They were perfectly joined, their bodies meshing together like the pieces of a puzzle.

Nothing had ever felt this right before.

"Please tell me you don't doubt this," he said, as if the question was of vital importance.

She closed her eyes and moved her hips. "Brit, not now."

He grabbed her head and kissed her mouth, then closed each eye. He held his lower body utterly still. "Tell me."

Tori thrust up against him, her inner muscles working down the length of his cock. "It doesn't matter."

"It does matter." His shoulders tensed under her fingers, and she could tell how much it was costing him not to move.

"I believe you," she whispered.

"Louder." He thrust once, nearly taking her over the edge, and pulled out.

"I believe you," she said, opening her eyes and grabbing his hips. She wrapped her legs around him and arched her back.

"Louder." He thrust again, leisurely this time, and bit her

nipple.

"Yes," she cried, "I believe you." Her hips moved wildly now, her inner muscles holding him fast.

"More," he demanded. "Tell me what you believe."

"I…" her eyes fluttered closed and her head began to thrash on the sheets as he began a slow, deep rhythm inside her. "I believe you want me."

"And you want me, too," he said, the rhythm increasing.

Her head was starting to spin and she was no longer sure what she was saying.

"God, I want you," she said, shuddering as they began to move together, bodies taking over where minds continued to struggle. "I need you!"

Released by her words, he buried his face in her neck and drove deeply inside her. It was hard and fast, but he made sure she was with him, screaming with pleasure before he finally abandoned himself and let out his own hoarse cry. Waves of rippling, soul-bending joy sent Tori's body into a cataclysm. She shuddered and lurched against him and he clutched her even tighter. For an endless moment, they abandoned themselves to the raging passion that controlled their bodies, and their minds.

• • •

Tori sat up in bed as Brit returned from the bathroom. His gaze lingered on her naked breasts and slim waist as she drew herself to standing and took a few steps away from the bed. Amazingly, he felt himself becoming aroused again, minutes after a bone-jarring orgasm.

Gently, he splayed his fingers over the curve of her hip and drew her against him. "Stay here tonight. I promise you won't be late to your meeting tomorrow."

Her emotions, usually so close to the surface, eluded him.

Velvety eyelids slid closed, her face a careful mask. "Maybe," she said. "I'll think about it."

Damn it, he was not going to allow her to take off. Not after what he'd felt when she moved underneath him. Surrendered to him. He tilted her face up and lightly kissed her mouth, starting first with that adorably plump lower lip, nibbling next on the edges. Her nipples hardened against his chest, and he smiled with satisfaction.

"Tori, my obstinate beauty, I'll set the alarm. I'll make you buttermilk pancakes and coffee in the morning. You can devour the paper. You're tired and need to get a good night's sleep." He peppered his words with kisses and then dropped down to take one rosy nipple into his mouth.

She took a sharp breath, then let it out unsteadily. "I'm having breakfast with Melissa."

"Then no pancakes." He rolled his tongue around the peak, slowly first, then again more quickly before turning to the other side.

"I think I would sleep better at the hotel," she said, her voice a breathy whisper.

"I'm considering tying you to the bed, but I'm not sure that's going to get me back in your good graces. You do forgive me, don't you?"

"Yes," she squeaked, as he applied gentle suction and started backing her toward the bed.

"Good. Because I only have a month before I leave. I would hate to waste any more of that time apologizing." Deliberately, he focused his attention on her breasts. At least he knew what to do with them. He sure as hell didn't know how to proceed with her.

He wanted to tell her how he couldn't stop thinking about her. How he called her office because he wanted to hear her voice. How every moment with her left him confused, turned on, and frustrated all at once. But how could he say that?

And even if he did, what would she say in return?

"A month for what?"

Tori's voice was flat, but the sudden pounding of her heart betrayed the emotion underneath.

"A month for this." Her knees hit the edge of the bed and she tumbled onto her back. He lowered himself beside her, guided her by the shoulder and waist onto her side, and then spooned their bodies together, stomach to back, joining them by as much warm skin as possible. Feeling like a teenage boy, he pressed his growing erection against her and looped his hands around to keep playing with the smooth skin of her breasts.

"Oh," she said.

Brit drew in a ragged breath. He hadn't been this nervous around a woman since…well, ever. He knew she didn't want anything serious, and of course, neither did he. But he couldn't imagine letting her walk away. Not now.

"I realize I sent us in the wrong direction, Tori, but can't we restart the clock? Start over from here?"

"For a month, you mean. Until you leave."

Her odd tone made him curse the position that did not allow him to see her face. Had he insulted her somehow? Was it too much, too fast? He licked his suddenly dry lips. Was that sweat forming on his brow?

What was he supposed to say?

"I know you said you don't do relationships, and I'm heading out of town so I thought…I'm not asking for a commitment. You don't have to worry about that."

"Of course not. Brit Bencher doesn't do commitments."

He had messed up. Gritting his teeth, Brit dropped his head against the back of her neck. Damn it!

"Tori, please stay with me." His voice was muffled by the fall of her hair.

Her heart had slowed back to a normal rhythm. That

could be good or bad.

"All right. But I'm not promising a month. I'm terribly busy at work right now. And we do live in different cities. We'll have to see how it goes."

Relief flooded him. He hadn't even realized until that point that his hands had tightened around her waist. He forced himself to relax and let her go.

"We'll take it one day at a time," he promised. "One day at a time."

• • •

Tori watched Brit's chest rise and fall as he drifted off to sleep, his breath coming in slow, even waves.

At times like this, she wished she could cry. She would storm around the bedroom, sobbing and throwing things like a fifties movie star. Her hair would flow in perfect waves around her face, and beautiful, crystal tears would course down her cheeks. She would tell Brit he was an ass of the first order, and he would drop on his knees and beg forgiveness.

But no tears came to her eyes. She wasn't a film star, or a model, or even a twenty-year-old ingénue. She was a twenty-something lawyer who had just sold her soul to the devil.

He was going to break her heart. Or perhaps it was already broken. Right now it was hard to tell. Something in her had soared that night when they made love. It had been different from anything she had experienced before—rough and yet so tender, unimaginable pleasure and then this pain. This aching pain for the relationship neither of them wanted, but her heart so desperately needed.

She wasn't so out of touch with her emotions not to recognize that. She needed him. She needed to feel this way. He had brought back to life a part of her she thought had died years ago. Wide-eyed and girlish, it was the part of her that believed in fairy tales and happy endings. It was the part of her that wanted to feel beautiful and sensual, not just smart and ambitious.

But he didn't want it. He wanted to have sex with her. She forced herself to say the word in her mind. He didn't want to make love—he wanted to have sex. And just for a month, after which he would leave and recapture the adolescent fantasy he'd been nursing all these years. She didn't doubt he needed it, just like she needed the fairy tales. The only difference was, he was going to get it, and she never would. There was no happy ending waiting at the end of this story.

All these years, with all the horrible men she'd dated, she thought her problem was her inability to connect deeply. She thought there was something wrong with her when Phil had broken off their engagement and all she'd felt was a vague sense of relief. But nothing could be further from the truth. She'd only known Brit for a matter of weeks, but in that short time he had penetrated her walls of protection and snuck past her formidable defenses. She was vulnerable, terrified, and unable to walk away.

She slid down farther under the covers and rested her hand on his hip. He was so perfectly male, so wonderfully hard and warm. His scent of brandy and spice flooded her senses.

He wanted her for a month.

One month.

And she had said yes.

Two weeks ago, she would have said no. No way would she let him drag her heart over a cliff. But things were different now. He had changed her with his touch, with the admission that he had wrung out of her in the heat of passion. She needed him. She needed to feel like a woman, even if only for a short time.

Tracing the outline of his thigh, Tori bowed her head

and accepted her decision. She had to see this thing through. Take the month she'd been given and enjoy every minute.

She knew he would break her heart. She knew in one month she'd be running back to the office, trying to repair the life that she'd always known. But she wasn't thinking about that now. Right now, she was opening herself to pleasure.

And to pain.

Chapter Seventeen

Gray metal filing carts filled with black binders and expandable folders lined the walls of the twentieth-floor conference room. The stale air reeked of take-out Chinese, coffee, and frustration. The team had already put in fifteen hours of work and everyone wanted to go home. But from the look on Karl Bulcher's face, home would not be in the cards any time soon. He had appeared in the office around seven, an unexpected visit for a Friday night, and now droned from the head of the conference table about the importance of this transaction, how he needed to know his team was dedicated and committed to putting aside everything else to make this deal happen.

It was either a disciplinary message or a pep talk. With Karl, there wasn't much of a difference.

Karl was short, with a round belly that could have been jolly had he worn it with a white beard and a twinkle in his eye. Instead, he clothed himself in dark suits and his eyes reflected nothing more than a hard, black stare. Tori had never seen him twinkle. He was cold and precise, rarely showing anger or excitement. When he was agitated, as he was now, he ground out his words as if he were biting through a piece of tough steak.

A buzz at Tori's hip signaled the arrival of a message. She eased the BlackBerry from its holster and opened the e-mail.

Are you in NYC?

It was Brit.

Stuck in a meeting. May not get out tonight. She glanced up and down as she wrote. Karl didn't like to be ignored. Though he expected his own messages to be returned instantly, regardless of where you were, he didn't like his meetings to be disrupted by people sending e-mails.

Unacceptable. This is our last weekend. I'll go there.

She almost dropped the device in her lap. Brit? Come to Philadelphia?

I might make it to NYC tomorrow, she wrote furiously.

Or you might not. I don't trust you.

Tori could not hide her smile. It had been three weeks since she'd made the decision to let Brit drag her heart off a cliff. They'd spent every weekend together. He sent her flowers and wrote stupid e-mails about his day. He made her laugh and blush, sometimes in the middle of the same meeting. They listened to jazz together and made love until dawn, when, exhausted and sated, they fell asleep in each others' arms.

But life hadn't disappeared, and Tori knew her ultimate commitment had to be to her job. Playing around with Brit was fun, perhaps even necessary. But work was her life. Work was the thing that would carry her after he'd left. Work would restore her after he'd lost interest and found someone new.

She wouldn't fall apart as her mother had, when her father left.

I can work on the train, she tapped furtively.

You'll end up in the office. Besides, you're desperate to

see me. You can't wait until tomorrow.

Unfortunately, that was true. Three weeks had only sharpened her desire for his lean body, and the company of his sharp mind.

Don't you have work to do?

I'm a short-timer. I don't do work anymore.

She snorted out loud at that one. Brit might be looking forward to his vacation, but he had a fierce loyalty to the company he had headed for ten years, and he had been working tirelessly to ensure it would be in good hands when he left.

"Tori? Do you have anything to add?" Karl glared at her through bushy gray brows and she jumped guiltily.

"What's that? Er, no. As usual, you said it all, Karl."

He narrowed his eyes at the compliment—Karl was nothing if not suspicious—and then turned immediately to expound on the epic responsibility that lay in the hands of everyone around the table.

That's it. I'm getting in the car. I'll see you in a few hours.

Tori's heart dropped. He was serious. She dug her nails into her palms and tried not to panic. At her insistence, they had spent all their weekends at Brit's place. Tori claimed she wanted to go to New York anyway, to see Melissa. The truth was that she didn't want Brit in her house. It would be too intimate, somehow, to have him there. His apartment was so clean, so sterile, it was like staying at a hotel. But her house… that was a different story.

I may not be home until ten or eleven.

I'm turning you off. I'll call you when I'm in Philadelphia.

Fretting over the thought of having Brit appear at her front door almost caused Tori to miss Karl's half question-half command:

"Now, Tori, why don't you bring us up to date on the efforts of your diligence team?"

Her fingers trembling with the need to write a stern message to Brit, convincing him to turn around immediately, Tori reluctantly pulled out the ten-page memo detailing each of the potential issues that could have significant repercussions on their acquisition strategy.

She ruthlessly pushed aside all thought of that crooked nose and absurdly broad shoulders barreling toward her in that damn black Mercedes. "I would love to."

The rest of the meeting was agony. Tori kept a tenuous hold on her emotions and managed to appear professional and competent—or so she hoped. When the lecture was over and the other lawyers had left the room to continue their work in their respective offices, Karl pulled Tori aside.

"Do you have a minute?" he asked, though he clearly expected she would.

"Of course," Tori said, her mind still spinning. She hadn't eaten at home all week, so the kitchen would be clean, but the laundry was another matter. Her hamper was overflowing, the towels hadn't been washed in ages, and who knew when she had last changed her sheets? Not to mention the layer of dust covering the mantle, the pictures on the walls, and the red ceramic mixer her mother had insisted should remain on the counter, in case either of them had the urge to make a loaf of bread.

That had been four years ago, when her mother was still able to cook. The appliance hadn't been used, or dusted, since. The whole house, really, belonged to her mother. Tori had only bought into the exclusive Chestnut Hill neighborhood because that's what Jeanne had always wanted. Tori could barely afford the payments, even on the cheapest house she could find, but it made Jeanne happy, and that's what mattered.

Selling the house now would have felt like a betrayal.

"What can I do for you, Karl? Did you have questions about the employee complaints?"

His already narrow lips tightened, and Tori felt the first flutter of panic. He did not look happy. Had he noticed her e-mailing during the meeting? Lord, she felt like a kid being called before the teacher for passing notes.

"Tori, I'm going to be straight with you. I don't think the team is working hard enough. Akro is seriously considering taking our work elsewhere."

She blinked, the words slowly registering in her brain. "I'm not sure I understand. Everyone on the team has made this matter a top priority. We've been working fifteen-hour days all month—some of our associates haven't taken a day off since June. The project is on track for the timeline you gave us. Is there something specific you are concerned about?"

He adjusted the navy blue pants that hung precariously a few inches below his impressive girth. If anything, his eyes grew colder. "I'm concerned about you, Tori. I came in last weekend and you weren't here. I tried to reach you in the office the weekend before that and you weren't here then either. To be perfectly frank, you're the only lawyer in at this firm I give a damn about, and I'm starting to question your dedication to this project."

"Nothing is more important to me than my work, Karl. You know that." Adrenaline made her voice quiver. Karl could not be unhappy with her work. He could not.

"I *used* to know that," he corrected. "Lately I've begun to wonder."

She swallowed hard. "Wonder about me?"

"Yes. It's not only the weekends. Even when you're in the office you don't seem as focused. When I got here tonight, you were sitting around chatting. I certainly hope that time isn't going to appear on my bill."

He was right—she had been joking with the other lawyers before he arrived. Usually they worked through dinner, but tonight someone had started talking about a bit they'd heard on *The Daily Show* and they had all started laughing. Before she knew it one of the associates had started doing horrible impressions, and they descended into pure silliness. They needed a break from the tension and it had felt wonderful. But Karl was right—it was out of character for her. Usually Tori didn't waste time on frivolity.

"We took a break for dinner. You can be assured I would never bill you for that."

He crossed his arms over his chest. "I expect to get 100 percent of your attention, Tori. I know plenty of other firms that can give me that attention if you aren't interested."

"I intend to deliver 100 percent, Karl." She straightened her shoulders and ignored the buzzing at her hip. "You won't be disappointed."

"I certainly hope not. As for the time line, we're going to need to move it up a few weeks. I've got other issues I need to address this fall and I want this deal wrapped up by then."

Move the schedule ahead a few weeks? The very thought of it made her knees go weak. She'd have to put everything else in her life on hold.

Everything.

"Of course." Tori nodded, and tried to keep her expression even.

"I'll see you tomorrow," Karl said.

"See you tomorrow," Tori echoed.

• • •

Brit turned on his phone as soon as he caught sight of downtown Philadelphia. He had hoped the drive from New York would give him time to clear his head, but he was as confused now as he had been when he left.

What to do about Tori?

He drummed his fingers on the steering wheel and shot

past a car dawdling in the fast lane.

Beautiful Tori.

Passionate, contrary, brilliant, driven Tori.

He was leaving in five days. Was it possible he would never see her again? Could he really walk away from her? In three short weeks, he'd gotten used to having someone to confide in, someone who would listen to his internal struggles without judgment. Someone who understood him better than he understood himself. Though she rarely confided back, his gut told him that she knew what it was like to feel trapped. Perhaps even more than he did.

She was, without a doubt, the most confusing female he'd ever come across. She resisted all attempts he'd made to drive their relationship deeper. Though he knew she visited her mother regularly at the nursing home, she never discussed it. When he tried to ask about her father, whose leaving had obviously had such a big influence on her, she made a joke and changed the subject. Sometimes he felt as if he understood her no better today than he had the first time they'd met.

Except that wasn't exactly true. He knew she had led Melissa through her interview with Solen with a combination of professionalism and wit that had instantly put Melissa at ease. A few days later, Melissa had been hard at work for Solen Labs, with a new passion and energy for life that Brit hadn't seen for years.

In three weeks he'd learned that Tori was smart and funny, and absolutely committed to those who wandered into her circle of protection. He'd learned that their bodies fit together like they were made for each other. She only needed to look at him with her melting brown eyes and he was at her feet, a slave to her pink lips and wickedly sensual hands.

Yes, he knew Tori, but it was despite her best efforts. It was as if she had erected a wall around her private heart, one he could breach only when they made love.

Which brought his thoughts around full circle. He was days from boarding a plane to Scotland, return date unknown, and his only regret would be leaving her behind. On the other hand, did he have a choice? She had made it clear she didn't want anything more than a short-term affair, and he was hardly going to offer his heart to someone who felt nothing in return. In some ways this weekend felt like a test, a final effort to break down the walls she had erected around her heart to see what, if anything, lay on the other side.

He hit number five on his speed dial.

Tori answered the phone. "Where are you?"

He smiled. She didn't mince words, his Tori. No "hello, sweetheart," or "can't wait to see you, darling."

"Entering Philly. I have directions; I called to let you know I was close."

"How did you get directions?" she asked suspiciously.

"Betsy. She e-mailed me earlier today because she knew you were going to be working late." Thank goodness for Tori's chatty, nosy, inappropriate secretary. She probably would have mailed him a key to Tori's house if he had asked.

Tori swore under her breath. "Look, I wish you'd kept your phone on. I'm going to have to work all weekend. You shouldn't have come down."

"You're not working all weekend," he said.

"Yes, I am."

"We'll talk about it when I get there. See you soon." He closed the phone over her protests. He'd heard her moan about work before. She always brought a stack of documents with her to New York, but with a few well-placed kisses, he'd been able to convince her to put them down.

It was their last weekend together and his last chance to move their relationship forward.

Tori was stubborn, but he wasn't called The Slayer for nothing.

Chapter Eighteen

Brit pulled to a stop in front of Tori's house and double-checked the address. The house, a small Tudor with peeling paint and a look of disrepair, stood out among the row of well-groomed lawns, large brick homes, and stone Colonials. She lived *here*? He imagined Tori in an apartment close to town, something close to takeout and good coffee—two things she claimed made life worth living. She should be in a vibrant area, full of other young, driven people. Instead, he found her in an old, wealthy neighborhood full of art galleries and antique stores. A place she didn't belong.

Brit jumped out and walked past the beds of wilted petunias and half-dead verbena that flanked the footpath to her front porch. This, at least, looked like Tori. She was far too busy to worry about her yard.

Tori opened the door as he charged up the front porch steps. She wore her oldest sweatshirt and a pair of soft cotton shorts.

He dragged her into his arms before she could open her mouth and gave her a deep kiss, instantly molding her body to his.

"You're not playing fair, darling," he murmured against her ear. "Those shorts should be illegal."

"They're an old pair of men's boxers," she said, swaying against him as his mouth dropped into the curve of her neck. "Stop kissing me. We need to talk."

"Can't we do both?" He slipped a hand under her sweatshirt and settled it on her hip, his thumb resting on the curve of her stomach. A familiar feeling. Her skin against his. Her mouth, yielding under the pressure of his lips.

How could he walk away from this?

"Brit, the door is open."

Without turning his head, he reached one foot behind him and kicked the door shut. "No it isn't," he said, and his hand moved higher, to touch one instantly erect nipple.

For a moment, Tori responded, as he knew she would. But then she straightened, her body becoming rigid. She pushed him away. "I'm serious. This isn't going to be a good weekend," she said.

"It's never a good weekend," Brit observed, only partly joking.

Recognizing the stubborn set to her jaw, he turned and examined Tori's home. The living room had a coved ceiling with a maple picture rail on the walls and maple trim around the doorways. A brick fireplace sat on one end of the room, flanked on either side by an old brocade sofa and matching love seat. Other than those pieces and a heavy old dining set, the house was bare. No rugs on the floor. No lamps or end tables. Unopened mail gathered in a pile on the dining room table, beside a bowl filled with plastic fruit. Built-in bookcases surrounded the fireplace, displaying a collection of Danielle Steele, Agatha Christie, and self-help books he knew she would never read.

"Are you sure you live here?" he said, raising a quizzical

brow.

"Of course I live here," she said crossing her arms over her chest. "What do you mean?"

"It just looks…"

"What?"

It looks sad. Lonely. Is this what you come home to every night?

His heart ached at the sight, but he knew he couldn't say anything. If there was one thing he had learned about Tori, it was that she couldn't tolerate pity.

He spread his hands in a gesture of helplessness. "Empty. Like no one lives here."

"Well that's a nice thing to say," she huffed, turning away.

"I don't mean to be insulting," he said. "It took me by surprise. It doesn't look like you."

Stiffly, she gestured toward the back of the house. "We took out the rugs and most of the furniture when my mother's balance started to fail. I don't have any money for renovations."

"Why don't we go upstairs?" he said, searching for a way to break the dark mood that hung over her.

"Fine." She threw back her hair and stomped up a narrow flight of stairs. The upstairs was a converted attic with a ten-foot ceiling along the ridgeline of the roof, tapering down at the eaves to three feet. Tori's bed sat at an angle to catch the morning sun. Brit relaxed at the sight. The room was an utter and complete disaster, but at least it felt like a home. Piles of laundry spilled out of a walk-in closet and littered the floor. A desk groaned under the weight of enormous piles of papers, files, and binders.

Hands on hips, Tori turned at the top of the stairs to face him. "So?"

Brit walked around slowly, flipping through a pile of papers on a bedside table, wiping dust off the edge of a framed picture of Tori and her mother, and then cautiously lowering himself onto the bed.

"Unlike some people, I don't have a live-in maid, you know," she added.

He patted the space next to him on the bed. "Sit with me."

"No."

He wanted to smile, but he knew that would make things worse. Oh, how he knew this woman. Her defensiveness. Her moods. The need that lay underneath the prickly exterior.

"Tori, I drove a hundred miles to see you. Can't I even get a 'hi, how are you?'"

She slumped down on the bed. "I know. I'm a frightful bitch. I'm sorry."

He eased her into his arms. "You've had a long day. I understand." After slipping off his shoes, Brit scooted back on the bed, and then guided her into position between his legs so he could rub her shoulders.

"Ohh…" Tori sighed with obvious pleasure.

"So, why don't you tell me what this is all about?"

She talked while he massaged, describing her interaction with Karl Bulcher, a man Brit would cheerfully punch if he ever saw. He let her get it all out, knowing where she was headed. "So you see," she finished, "I have to be there tomorrow morning. I don't have a choice about this, Brit. And I need to be focused. I can't afford to spend the weekend thinking about you."

"Thinking about me?" He pulled her tightly against him. Her back nestled against his chest and his chin dropped on top of her head. "Why would you do a thing like that?"

"Because you keep sending me e-mails," she managed to retort. "How am I supposed to get any work done? It's very distracting, you know."

"You are a piece of work, sweetheart," Brit said

admiringly. "You keep fighting until the bitter end."

"I'm serious," she said. "You should stay at a hotel tonight. That way I won't wake you up in the morning."

"At some point I'm going to start taking this personally."

"Well, you should," Tori pushed back into a sitting position, and then heaved herself out the bed.

"Come with me," he said suddenly, the words falling, unbidden, from his lips.

"Where? To a hotel? Haven't you heard a word I said? I need to work tomorrow." She punctuated each word slowly and distinctly. "If I don't work, Karl leaves the firm. I lose my most important client, and probably kill any hope of partnership in the process."

"No. Not to a hotel. To Scotland."

Chapter Nineteen

"Scotland?" Tori's mouth dropped open. She couldn't believe what he'd said. "Brit, I can't even take off the weekend. How am I going to go to Scotland?"

"You're a fourth-year associate at a law firm, Tori, not the president of the United States. Take the week to wrap things up. Or if you're really concerned about it, take two weeks and meet me there."

Tori's entire body twitched with a combination of shock and anger. "Good to know you think I'm completely expendable."

"I didn't mean that," Brit said. "Of course you'd be missed. They'd have to hire three associates to replace you."

She knew he was trying to defuse her temper with humor, but she had no interest in being mollified. The very idea of her going to Scotland was ridiculous, and Brit knew it.

She spun around on her heel and started down the stairs. "I'm getting myself a cup of tea, and then I'm going to bed. By myself."

She padded down the stairs. Brit followed a few paces

behind.

When they reached the kitchen, he leaned against a counter, watching as she strode across the room to grab the old metal teakettle. His deep voice echoed in the empty room. "You won't even consider it?"

Tori paused, her fingers tightening around the handle of the kettle. "I can't. I told you what Karl said tonight. I slack off, he leaves the firm. I can't risk that."

The amusement left Brit's voice. "Yes, you can. In fact, if you don't start risking it, I'm afraid you're going to lose something far more important than your job."

Tori's heart fluttered. She filled the kettle and set it on the stove, then grabbed a cup and a tea bag from the cupboard by the sink. Her cell phone rang from the living room but she ignored it. Probably Karl, making sure she was still working. "What's that supposed to mean?" she asked.

"Look around you, Tori. Think about it. You're living in an empty house, spending every minute you aren't sleeping at work. How do you expect to have any friends? How are you ever going to have any relationships?"

She stared at him, her mouth dropping open in astonishment. "You *just* figured this out about me? Brit, I do what I have to do to make partner. That's all. That's what I'm living for."

"But that makes no sense!" He pushed off the counter and stalked toward her. "You are a beautiful, intelligent, vibrant woman. Why do you punish yourself this way?"

"You may not know this," Tori retorted, "but some of us need our jobs. Some of us need to know that when the bill comes from the nursing home, they'll have the money to pay it."

"I get that, I do." Brit ran his fingers through his hair in frustration. "I don't get the *way* you do it. You treat everything that's not work like it's an annoyance. A distraction from what really matters."

The emotions were coming too quickly for Tori to catalog. She reacted without thinking, the words spilling out in an unplanned, uncontrollable rush. "We had nothing, Brit. Absolutely nothing. My father left my mother with an overdrawn checking account, a high school diploma, and an eight-year-old kid. She worked harder than any person you've ever met, and now she's in a nursing home, and she doesn't remember her own name. I won't risk her life. I won't."

"Tori..." Brit reached out to touch her shoulder but she jerked away. He ignored her and reached out again, this time turning her to face him. "Tori, you can't go back and fix things for your mother. I don't care how successful you are. It won't change what she went through."

"No. It won't. But I sure as hell can make sure I don't repeat her mistakes."

"Ah. I see." Brit dropped his hand. "You're determined to cast yourself as your mother, and me as your father. You refuse to accept the possibility that maybe there's a man out there who's worth taking a chance on. And yes, I know I didn't exactly start out the right way, but things have changed. At least, they have for me."

Tori's throat caught. "What changed?"

"I don't want you for a month, Tori. I thought that would be enough but it isn't. I want more. I want to rub your shoulders as you fall asleep. I want to cook you breakfast in the morning. I want you to come away with me because you can see that work isn't the most important thing in the world."

Her mother's voice echoed in Tori's head. *Before you trust a man, Tori, ask yourself, Where will you be if he leaves you? How will you keep going after he's gone?*

"I'm sorry," she said. "Work *is* the most important thing to me. I can't afford to take this weekend off. Not for anyone."

He threw up his hands in frustration. "So that's it? You're

ready to give it all up for a weekend in the office?"

"Give what up? Give up a short-term affair with a man who is running away from his own life and trying to reclaim his lost youth? Sorry if that doesn't sound more promising than a lifelong career." Tori knew she was lashing out at him, perhaps unfairly, but it seemed vitally important that he stop looking at her with those solemn, sad eyes. He needed to feel a little of the heartbreak that was enveloping her.

"I screwed up a lot of things in my life, Tori. I worked too hard for too long. I tried to order around my family like they were a bunch of unruly kids. I'm lucky they didn't disown me. But I'm ready to start over. *You're* determined to stay here in this empty, hollow house, running in your hamster wheel, terrified to let anyone into your life. Who's running away? Me, or you?"

"You knew what I had to offer," Tori said, closing her mind to any further attacks. "We said one month, no commitments. I kept my end of the bargain."

"Well, I didn't." Brit looked around the room, and Tori could feel him cataloging the dust on the appliances, and the stack of dishes in the sink. "I wasn't ready to walk away from you. That's why I asked you to come to Scotland. But now I wonder if maybe I was wrong. Maybe you don't want to start over. Maybe I *should* walk away."

"Please, go right ahead," Tori said, her heart breaking in tiny, tingling pieces. "It isn't as though I wasn't expecting it."

"If I leave, I'm not coming back," Brit warned, his dark brows pulled together, his eyes boring into her as if they could see into her very soul. "You say I'm trying to reclaim my lost youth, and maybe that's true. I wasn't happy with the life I was living, and I'm starting something new. I want you to come with me, but I understand if that's not possible."

Tori's entire body felt as if it had become a single, open wound. She stifled a cry of pain. "You're not playing fair.

You've got a perfect family, and a job, and money, and it's all waiting for you when you come back." She slammed down her cup on the counter, her entire body trembling with restrained emotion. "You've got everything to come back to and I've got nothing, Brit. Nothing but Goddamn Karl Bulcher!"

Brit paused. "You're right. You're absolutely right."

Tori blinked. "What? You mean…"

"I mean, I can't ask you to give that up." He strode forward and pulled her into a quick embrace. "You need to get some sleep. I'll stay at a hotel tonight. You won't hear from me again. I hope things work out for you, Tori. I really do."

Then, as quickly as he had come, Brit turned around and left.

. . .

So you gave her the ultimatum and she turned you down.

Brit drove away from Tori's house feeling like he'd ripped out his own heart. When he'd walked into that house and seen how she'd been living, he should have known the answer to his question. Of course she wouldn't come away with him.

Tori's scars went far deeper than he'd imagined. It would take a bulldozer to get her away from her job.

He forced himself to keep driving, even though every muscle in his body screamed at him to turn around. He was done trying to fix people. He had reached out to her and she'd pushed him away. He had to move on. It wasn't as if they were married. They weren't even dating, according to Tori. He'd tried to change the boundaries of their relationship—if one could even call it that—and she'd said no.

End of story.

So why did he feel like walking out her door was the biggest mistake he'd ever made?

Chapter Twenty

Chest heaving, despair clawing at her throat, Tori watched Brit drive away. The phone began to ring even as the enormity of what had happened settled like a cold weight on her shoulders. The terrible, painful things he had said swirled in her mind. She walked back to the living room in a daze, barely registering the fact that the answering machine had picked up.

"Miss Anderson? This is Chad from Langston Estate. Can you please call me as soon as possible? Thanks."

She froze. A horrible rush of terror left her momentarily dizzy. Struggling with a wave of nausea, she bolted to the phone and picked it up, but it was too late. With trembling fingers, she hit the speed dial and heard Chad's voice on the other line.

"Chad? This is Tori."

"Tori, I'm so sorry." His voice was warm and soft, as if he meant to envelop her in a blanket. "So very sorry."

She knew what he was going to say. Sinking down on the floor in the middle of the living room, she pressed a trembling hand to her forehead. "What happened?" she managed to say, the words coming from a great distance.

She recalled her cell phone ringing while she fought with Brit. Chad had never called her before, on either her cell or landline.

"We aren't sure. They think perhaps a stroke. We found her in her bed this evening. You had a DNR, so they didn't try to revive her."

He kept talking then, about a death certificate and the funeral arrangements, how she should come down to say good-bye before they had to move the body. How they had paperwork on file that said she wanted to be cremated and was that still what Tori wanted. And all she could do was nod and breathe. Nod and breathe. Until the breathing became too difficult and she had to say a muffled good-bye and throw down the phone and suck in air like she was drowning.

Panic started next, panic in thick, heavy waves that curled her fingernails into her palm until the pain in her hand startled her into release. With an effort she stood up, grabbed her keys, and walked outside.

She needed to go to Langston. To say good-bye to the empty shell of the woman who had once been her mother. The only person who understood why she worked the way she did. The only person who would have appreciated the sacrifice she had just made.

The space in front of the house looked empty without Brit's sleek black car. Her Mini sat at the end of the driveway, and she walked over to it, staring down at the pile of documents sitting on the passenger seat.

She should read them tonight. Maybe she could bring them to Langston. She'd spent enough time around doctors to know that they always kept you waiting. Even to pronounce death, surely they would keep her waiting. No sense wasting time.

The thought brought a rush of bile to her throat. Was Brit right? Had she lost her soul completely? Her mother lay dead and all she could think of was work?

Where were the tears?

What had she become?

• • •

The moon had set and the night sky filled with stars when Tori stumbled back into the house, her head spinning, her breath coming in a thin whistle through clenched teeth. The nervous rhythm of her heart pounded through her sweatshirt, but still no tears clogged her throat.

She was a monster. She'd sat through hours of shoulder patting and sorrowful looks, said good-bye to her mother's calm, peaceful face, and still her eyes remained dry. Perhaps that was because the frail, white-haired body did not look like it belonged to the woman who had raised her. Over the past year, she had gotten used to thinking Jeanne's body housed a nervous stranger. It was hard to believe she was really saying good-bye.

In some ways, she had said good-bye a long time ago. In other ways, she wasn't sure she ever could.

Tori retraced her steps up the porch and into the house, moving without thinking toward her mother's bedroom. She threw open the closet doors and buried her face in her mother's clothes, which still bore the faint smell of the heavy perfume she loved. From the floor of the closet Tori retrieved pairs of shoes, and tossed them in a pile in the middle of the room. For a moment, she held each one individually, imagined the shoe on her mother's foot, and imagined her mother in the room, straightening her stockings as she got ready for work.

It was time to clean out the room. Her mother was never

coming back.

A roaring sound in her ears made it difficult to concentrate, but the tears still would not come. She began to shiver, suddenly as cold as she had ever been before, her legs covered with goose bumps, her body frigid under her clothes.

Lurching to her feet, her body shaking, Tori yanked back the covers of the bed and huddled under a thin wedding ring quilt. Once, Tori had seen Jeanne crying into this quilt, great hulking sobs she could not hide from her young daughter. It was soon after her father had left them, when Jeanne was still trying to pretend she could keep it all together, and her heart hadn't been ripped out and left for dead. Now, as Tori wrapped the quilt around her shaking body, she remembered that dark time, her fear that her mother would never regain her sanity and that she, Tori, would never be loved or safe, ever again.

Tonight, after she viewed the body, the counselors at Langston had sat down with Tori. They told her grief could take many forms. They said when an Alzheimer's patient dies, the family may feel relief that the struggle is over, and then guilt for having such a feeling. Tori understood that, had even expected it.

But they hadn't told her about the cold.

They hadn't mentioned the feeling that her breath would be forever stolen from her chest, her lungs perpetually half-filled, her body wrapped in sheets of ice. When she exhaled into the quilt, her breath created a tiny pocket of warmth, and she pressed her cheek against it.

Her mother had always loved this room. She said this house made up for all those years when they'd lived in tiny apartments without any soul. She thought the flowered wallpaper, beautiful woodwork, and fifties linoleum had soul. Even if Tori always felt like a visitor here, her mother felt at home, and that's what had mattered. All her life, the only thing that had really mattered was trying to make up for all the hurt her mother had suffered.

And now she was gone.

Her gaze fell on the nightstand, where a small leather-bound book sat by a lamp with a ceramic base decorated with soft blue forget-me-nots and tiny pink roses.

Pushing herself to sitting, Tori took the battered volume off the table. The smell of leather and musty pages emerged as pulled back the cover and flipped through the worn pages. The first page was dated eight years before, when Tori had first bought the house. It was a diary, in her mother's unmistakable loopy handwriting.

Feeling like an interloper, but unable to put it down, Tori began to read. At first, she huddled under the blankets, struggling for breath and warmth, but something about the process of reading soothed her. The sound of her mother's voice, echoing in her ear, eased the pressure on her chest.

Most of the early entries focused on Jeanne's struggle to accept her diagnosis.

"I'm keeping this journal because they tell me it's good to write, to keep your mind active. It terrifies me, the thought of what that means, so here I am, writing away..."

Many of the pieces were short accounts of daily life, of places she had been and worried she would forget. Others were complaints—about her nurse, her medications, and especially the restrictions Tori placed on her from cooking, from driving, and eventually from leaving the house by herself.

Tori skimmed most of it quickly, lingering only for a moment on the passages filled with good memories before moving on to what came next. There was a rhythm to the writing, good days mixed with bad, handwriting slowly losing its shape and the entries becoming shorter over the years.

The dates were sporadic—for a few weeks she'd write every day, and then months would go by without an entry.

Toward the back of the book, an entry caught her eye. The pages were watermarked and the writing smeared. Tori sat up and spread the pages of the book as she read. It began,

Tori is working late again tonight, and the house seems dark and empty. I wish there was some way I could tell her how lonely I am. But I don't want to burden her more than she already is...

Tori closed her eyes and took a shuddering breath. Steeling herself, she opened her eyes and stared back down at the painful words.

I can't help but think that this is partly my fault. After Thad left, I worried about everything. I worried about paying the bills. I worried about being able to send her to college. And I missed him so much it was like a hole in my heart. I know I overreacted. I tried to steer Tori away from men who would be like him and to push her to focus on her career. And I still believe that I did the right thing. I'm so proud of her, of how hard she works and how successful she's been. But at some point I forgot that the most important thing was that she was happy. Is she happy now? Is she happy with Phil? I don't know but somehow I can't help but think that I failed her. I only wish I could talk to her about this. I try and try but the words will never come. Oh, how I wish the words would come!

A scratchy, sandpaper feeling tickled the back of Tori's throat. She cleared it, but everything had become tight and thick.

Two months later, she stopped at another entry:

I can't help but wonder if someday Tori will read this. Tori, if you do read this, I hope you aren't mourning for me, but know that I am in a better place. I hope you know that I loved you with all my heart and every ounce of my being. I hope that I didn't send you down the wrong path. I hope that you know how proud I am of you. I hope you could feel my love, even if I could never say it. I hope most of all that you don't make the same mistakes that I made. I hope that you are happy.

Tori closed the book and hugged it to her heart. An unfamiliar wetness rolled down her cheeks and she pushed it aside with the faded quilt. But it kept coming and coming, until painful noises rattled in her chest. Finally, she dropped her head into her hands and sobbed.

Chapter Twenty-One

Tori threw her purse down on the conveyor belt, removed her shoes, and threw them into a gray plastic tub. After pushing both into the X-ray machine, she walked through the security gate and was relieved not to hear the buzz of the metal detector.

"Have a nice flight, ma'am," the burly TSA agent said with a polite nod.

"Thanks." She snatched her purse and shoes and pulled the wrinkled boarding pass from her back pocket. Gate E5. She squinted at the glowing departure screen to make sure the gate hadn't changed and then set off at a grim pace.

E23…E22…adrenaline had already sent her pulse through the roof and she began to pant. Had it really been a week since her mother died? Was it possible that so much time had elapsed? It seemed as if she'd been living in an alternate universe since then, with time moving slower and faster all at the same time.

E18…E17…what would he think when he saw her there? Would he even speak to her? Had she truly lost him forever when he walked out her door?

E10...E9...E8.

Tori hitched her bag over her shoulder and began to jog. She was going to throw up. She needed to get this over with, and she refused to have this conversation on a plane to England. Though she had bought the ticket, she didn't intend to use it unless he wanted her there. Really wanted her there.

She was moving so fast that she almost plowed into the tall, broad-shouldered man in a dark blue polo shirt and faded blue jeans, walking away from the gate. Blue-black hair curled obediently back from his forehead. Tori caught her breath when she saw the familiar crooked nose.

"Brit." The words died in her throat. For a moment she considered turning around and running back the other direction. But she had come too far, learned too much about herself in the week since her mother's death to do any such thing. Squaring her shoulders, she cleared her throat and tried again.

"You're going the wrong way," she said.

He drew back when he saw her, shock widening his eyes. "Tori? What are you doing here?"

His eyes were guarded, the gray sky of a snowy day. Better not to think about what that meant, she thought. Better to simply press on without thinking.

"Do you have a minute? I have something I need to tell you."

He cocked his head, studying her from head to toe. "I was about to get on a plane. Are you sure it will only take a minute?"

"My mother died," she blurted out. "Right after you left. It was a massive stroke."

He drew back. "Jesus, I'm sorry. I had no idea."

"Of course you didn't. How could you?"

He inclined his head toward a row of seats. "Perhaps we

should sit down?"

"I think I better stand up," she said, a nervous smile creasing her lips. "I may need to pace."

"I see." He took her elbow and steered her away from the crowd. "I'm sorry, Tori. I really am."

Polite. He sounded excruciatingly polite and concerned. The kind of concern you'd have for a stranger. She bit her lip.

"I would have called to tell you but I didn't want to do it over the phone, and it was impossible to get away."

Something flickered in those inscrutable eyes. He adjusted a brown leather satchel on his shoulder and started to turn away. "Of course. You could hardly use your mother's death as an excuse to take a few days off. Listen, I don't mean to seem unfeeling but I've got to get on my plane."

"No, no." She grabbed his elbow and spun him back to face her. "I did take a few days off, mostly because I was crying so hard I couldn't see the ground in front of me. But then I had to go in to make contingency plans."

"Contingency plans? For what?"

"For my quitting." She took a deep breath. "I quit my job. I realized something. I realized a lot of things. I realized that I've been using my job as an excuse not to let myself care about anything. My mom had me so scared that I'd be deserted by someone I loved that I wasn't loving at all. I dated men I didn't care about so they couldn't hurt me. Hell, I didn't even care about my fiancé—I was more upset when my cat left me than when he did!"

Brit's mouth twitched at the corner. "Your cat left you?"

She brushed it aside. "Long story."

"You'll have to tell me about it sometime."

Was that a crack? A hint of emotion in his blank facade? Encouraged, she pressed on.

"I thought if I made partner, then I'd have finally done what she wanted, and she'd be happy and I'd be able to relax.

But it wouldn't have been enough. That's what I realized. It would never have been enough. When I met you, Brit, I was starving, and I didn't even know it. I thought maybe I could satisfy my hunger by sleeping with you, but that only made it worse. Because along the way, despite all my efforts, I fell in love."

Wringing her hands together, she forced herself to look at him, full and square in the face, holding nothing back. "I love you, Brit. I know you don't feel the same way, and maybe never will. But I'm tired of giving up before I start. I'm tired of spending more time with my damn BlackBerry than the only person in the world who makes me feel alive. I want to go to Scotland with you, if the offer still stands."

He didn't respond. His face had frozen into an expressionless mask.

Unable to bear the sudden silence, Tori hurried on. "You probably don't want anything to do with me right about now. I know when you left you said you weren't coming back and I understand if you don't want me to come now that you know how I feel. But I had to tell you. Even if you don't love me back, I still want to be with you. Pathetic, huh?" She tried for a smile, but it came out pinched, scared. "I had to tell you. I had to take a chance that you wouldn't push me away."

He blinked and set down his bag. He opened his mouth, but no words came out.

Once again, Tori sailed into the void. "Look, I can see how you feel. They're boarding first class now. You better go." She turned, her legs trembling so badly she wondered if she would make it thirty feet, let alone all the way back to Philadelphia.

His hand closed around her arm. "Stop. Stop for one minute. You lawyers spend so much time talking I think you forget how to listen."

"Well that's uncalled for," she said. "I listen plenty. And

besides, I'm not a lawyer anymore. I don't now what I am, exactly, but it isn't a lawyer."

"You'll be a lawyer until the day you die, my love."

"No I won't. Did you hear me? I quit my job. As in quit, terminate—" The sound of the endearment finally penetrated her brain, and her mouth fell open. "What did you call me?"

"I thought you said you were a good listener."

She punched him in the arm. "Don't you dare tease me, you oaf!"

A tender smile curved his lips. "I wouldn't dream of it. You'd have me for breakfast."

"If you call me a tough nut, I'm turning around and walking right back out of this airport," she said, voice quavering, tears filling her eyes. She had cried more in the past week than she'd ever thought possible. Once the dam broke, the tears seemed to linger behind her eyes, reappearing at a moment's notice.

"You've got me over a barrel then, counselor. Because I would do anything to keep that from happening."

That was when the first hint of cautious optimism hit her. Like a flower stretching its petals toward the warmth of an early morning sun, she let her body sway toward him. "Why?"

"Because I love you, too." He wrapped his arms around her, lifting her up so their eyes were on the same level, and her feet dangled helplessly above the floor. "I realized it that night at your house when you stood in that kitchen, surrounded by your mother's things but so determinedly yourself. You're belligerent and temperamental. You make me laugh and you make me think. You understand me better than anyone. Do you know, before you came along, I didn't even realize I don't like my apartment? It's a beautiful place, but it's not me. I want a house, like you have—except with more furniture, and maybe a few rugs."

Tori smiled through her tears, as Brit continued. "I want

a dog and a family. I want you, darling. Leaving you that night was one of the hardest and stupidest things I've ever done. I thought I could bully you into caring about me. When you turned me away, I thought I had lost you forever."

He leaned his face against her cheek as she wrapped her arms around his neck. "I wasn't going to get on the plane. I couldn't. I was coming back to find you, to beg you to give me one more chance. We've both been living someone else's life, Tori. What do you say we start living our own? Together?"

Her heart, struggling to comprehend what he had already said, fluttered unsteadily. "What do you mean?"

He lowered her to the ground and pressed tiny kisses on her eyes, her nose, and her lips. "We can start with Scotland. I need a vacation and I think you do, too. When we're ready to come back we can find a new place—a house somewhere that doesn't look like your mother's or like my sisters decorated it. It will look like us. You can practice law, but I promise to interfere whenever you start working more than sixty hours a week."

"And what about you?"

Brit shrugged. "I'm not sure what I'll do. Maybe I'll find someone like your friend Jerry who needs help starting up a new company. It wasn't until I talked to you and Jerry that I realized that was what I missed. My passion is starting from scratch and building something out of nothing. I'd like to do that again. Then again, we'll have a wedding to plan, so that will take some time. Of course we could elope, but I think my family would kill us—"

She hit him on the arm. An enormous, ridiculous smile threatened to split her face in half even as fat, watery tears slid down her cheeks. "Don't you dare think you're going to get away without proposing to me, you cretin."

Without missing a beat he dropped onto one knee. "Tori Anderson, love of my life, I have no ring to slip on your finger.

I have no job and a lousy apartment that feels like a movie set. The only thing I have to offer is my heart and my love. Will you accept?"

A fresh wave of tears welled up in her eyes. "Oh yes. Yes!"

He jumped to his feet and kissed her with all the passion and love she never thought she'd have. The tears slid down her cheeks, healing her, making her whole.

"We will create something new together," he said. "Just the two of us."

She nodded and held him close. Tori's Rules of Negotiation Number Six: When you're offered the deal of a lifetime, smile. And never let it go.

Acknowledgments

I couldn't have written this book if I hadn't spent a decade in the trenches of law and business, where, unlike Tori, I had the benefit of many mentors, friends, and understanding clients. I can't begin to name all the people who supported me during my years of practice, through the ups and downs of bed rest, babies, illness, long days, and lots of takeout, but to each of you, I offer my grateful thanks. Special acknowledgments always go to my critique partner, the ever-patient and long-suffering Susan Sey, who reads everything I write and still returns my e-mails. To my sister Maia, my advocate and best friend, thank you for giving Tori the ethical green light to date Brit. She couldn't have done it without you. Though it makes me uncomfortable to even imagine him reading this book, I have to send love out to my incredibly supportive father, who wants nothing to do with romance novels but would probably read this if I asked (don't worry, Dad, I won't!). And finally, to my darling husband, who knows I am a lawyer down to my toes and loves me anyway, I can only say this: I am a very lucky lady.

About the Author

Inara wrote her first book when she was fifteen—a romance called "A Wild and Stormy Passion" that featured swordplay, a pirate heroine, and plenty of naughty bits (all of which came entirely from her imagination). Since then, she's written romances of the category, contemporary, and fantasy varieties. Her books are sinfully sensual and deeply emotional. Inara reserve the right to enjoy country music, puppies, and love-at-first sight. When she's not writing, she enjoys to spending time wandering around in the woods and has been known to occasionally dress up her little white dog in princess costumes.

Discover more category romance titles from Entangled Indulgence...

OVER HER WED BODY
a novel by Alexia Adams

Beckett Samuelson can spot a gold digger when he sees one. So when his ailing father announces his engagement to the private nurse he's only known for two months, Beckett has to step in. Before long he realizes he realizes she's the perfect next Mrs. Samuelson. If only he was the intended groom...

HOW NOT TO MESS WITH A MILLIONAIRE
a Mediterranean Millionaires novel by Regina Kyle

Interior decorator Zoe Ryan's life resembles a country song. What's a girl to do? Leave everything behind for a bit...in Italy. When she gets there, she finds a surprise—millionaire restaurateur Dante Sabbatini in the kitchen. In his underwear. Making coffee. It's suddenly not only hot outside... but what is he doing inside, in her temporary kitchen? The very thing, it seems, that she's trying to avoid, and resisting is impossible.

NO PLAYER REQUIRED
a Biggest Little Love Story novel by JoAnn Sky

Billionaire casino magnate Rafael "Rafa" Salord is forced to exchange caviar for cowboy boots when he's sent to "grow up" and run his father's newly acquired casino in the middle of nowhere downtown Reno. When he crosses paths with feisty Destiny Morson, he starts to wonder if that nonsense about love-at-first-sight might actually be true. Maybe it's time to trade in his playboy status and bet on something more.